THE LAST MAGNOLIA

BY

DENNIS R. MAYNARD

BOOK TEN

DIONYSUS PUBLICATIONS

Dionysus Publications
49 Via del Rossi
Rancho Mirage, California 92270

Email Orders & Comments: Episkopols@aol.com
Telephone: 760.324.8589
ISBN: **9781091089846**

www.Episkopols.com

Dionysus Publications
Books for clergy and the people they serve.

THE LAST MAGNOLIA
(BOOK TEN)

All your favorite characters have returned for your tenth visit to First Church and Falls City, Georgia.

Bishop Sean Evans and his partner, Rabbi Eze Dolan, face new threats of being outed.

Colonel Mitchell rallies a large group of supporters to attack the ministry of Father Steele Austin.

Chadsworth Purcell Alexander reaches out to Steele for help and risks having his identity exposed.

Steele and Randi must decide how to punish Virginia Mudd Willoughby.

The Reverend Melvin and Judith MacClaren return to Falls City and raise over a million dollars in one night.

Elmer Idle and Rose MacClaren receive a wonderful surprise.

Steele and his good friend, The Reverend Josiah Williams, confront an act of racism directed at them.

Almeda Alexander Drummond hosts a wedding reception you don't want to miss.

And, **Virginia Mudd Willoughby** lives in fear that her husband will discover her secret sins.

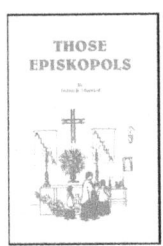

**Those
Episkopols**

**Forgive & Get Your
Life Back**

**The Magnolia Series
(10 Books)**

**When Sheep
Attack**

**Preventing A
Sheep Attack**

**Healing For Pastors
and People
Following A Sheep Attack**

Even Jesus Needed Money

FOR SPECIAL OFFERS
AND
VOLUME DISCOUNTS,
ORDER DOCTOR MAYNARD'S BOOKS
AT:
www.Episkopols.com

This one is for Nancy Anne.

COVER DESIGN

I am grateful to Chris Koonce of Fort Worth, Texas, for designing the cover for this book. He is a very talented young artist. Chris earned a Bachelor of Fine Arts degree in 1991 from the University of North Texas. I encourage you to visit his website to view his portfolio of artwork. There are several opportunities for personalized gifts for yourself and others. He can also be a resource for fundraising opportunities for your organization, parish, or school. Please visit his website at:

www.kcfunart.com

ALSO
ON YOU TUBE AT KCFUNART

FORWARD

In the forward to **Book Two** I wrote, "The beautiful thing about a novel is that the reader gets to look inside the various personalities that come to life on its pages. We get to see their hurts, their fears, their secrets. We literally get an emotional MRI of their inner selves. We gain insight into the very things that motivate them to do the things that they do."

It may have been a bit naive but I wanted to believe that through the characters in these novels, we could get to know, understand, accept, and love those in our own worlds that differ from us. I wanted to utilize fictional characters in a novel to help my readers look beyond stereotypical labels to see the soul of the person living with it.

I wanted the parables in these novels to transform both our thinking and our actions. *Once upon a time there was this poor black couple that wanted to buried in a segregated cemetery.* Hear this parable, *in a certain community there was a homeless man that at one time had a family.* Or, learn from the following parable. *A wealthy closeted gay man feared his secret would destroy him.*

I had hoped that if my readers could only embrace the characters revealed on these pages, they might then be able to translate that acceptance and affection to similar people in their own world. Since writing the first book in this series, *Behind The Magnolia Tree,* I've discovered such an endeavor is not as easy as I'd hoped. I have even failed with some.

I've lost a few readers, and in some cases friends. These readers found a couple of the characters I illuminated and their story lines to be repugnant, even sinful. One by one, I've received the letters and comments from those that found my efforts offensive, even contrary to the Scriptures.

I'd believed that by living in the glass house with Father Steele and Randi Austin we would be better able to love and appreciate the ministries of our own clergy and their families. Once again, there were those that dismissed their fictional story as exactly that.

I tried to pull back the ugly veil that most every pastor in all religions lives with on a daily basis. In every congregation there are a handful that believe they have been called by God to make their pastor's life miserable. Here again, I have failed. There are those that refuse to believe that anyone could be that cruel to a member of the clergy.

This is *Book Ten* in the series. I am more determined than ever to push onward. Perhaps if you know a little more about me you'll understand what motivates me. My father was one of sixteen children. My mother was one of twelve. I am one of six. I became an uncle when I was still a toddler. In the neighborhood where I grew up my grandparents, three maternal aunts, and four maternal uncles literally lived within blocks of our home. On my mother's side of the family I have fifty-two first cousins. I've lost count of the number of cousins I have from my father's fifteen siblings. I started kindergarten with several of my first cousins and graduated high school with all of them twelve years later. Family picnics on Sundays and holidays often numbered well over one hundred people.

If you were to come to one of those picnics, it would look like a gathering of the United Nations. In my family circle several Native American tribes are represented. There are Cherokees, Creeks, and Navajos. We have family members from Puerto Rico, India, and Mexico. Other family members come from Norway, Germany, Italy, England, Poland, France, and Ireland. Our family includes African Americans and *Lily White Caucasians*. We have gays and lesbians. There are Primitive Baptists, Pentecostals, Evangelicals, Mormons, Methodists, Roman Catholics, and a sprinkling of Episcopalians.

The point is this. Growing up in such a large and multifarious family allowed me to experience diverse people loving one another. My family does. While part of the family professes to be *Yellow Dog Democrats,* there is another branch that was born with the word *Republican* imprinted on their original birth certificates. Disagree? You bet we do on occasion. Debate politics? We do so especially around election time. But family is family and that's more important than anything else. I often say that our tribe motto is *Nada es mas importante que la familia.*

I am also a child of the sixties. I attended high school, college, and graduate school during that glorious decade. I went to the rallies. I marched in the demonstrations. I sat on the gymnasium floors in colleges and universities and sang the songs. I did more than sing the songs of the sixties. I believed the lyrics. I wanted to dream of a world without war. I knew that it's possible to love people for who they are and not because of their label, fame, station in society, wealth, or lack thereof.

And finally, I am a product of The Episcopal Church. I chose this church to be my church back in those same sixties. I continue to admire her for her courage. When it is needed she speaks prophetically against bigotry and prejudice in any form. She routinely devotes resources to helping the poor and disenfranchised. More recently she has dared to change the paradigm strangling the Historic Episcopate and now includes women in the apostolic line. She has opened her arms to all and welcomed them home.

While I've failed to change the hearts and minds of some that have picked up one of these novels, I'm grateful that you have remained with me. I thank you for loving the outcasts, the elite, the saints, and the sinners that live in Falls City, Georgia. I am most grateful to you for introducing my work to your friends, family, and fellow church members.

I pray you've witnessed the power of God's grace in the lives of the good folks that call Falls City, Georgia home. In these books you've seen those that we loved to hate become characters we've learned to love. Acts of mercy that received great opposition have flourished. It's the eternal story of redemption. It's the story of Jesus. If you are able to see the Gospel Story being lived out in these ten novels, then that makes it all worthwhile.

I hope you will enjoy this visit to First Church. I pray you'll see God working through the ministry and lives of the people in this place.

Once again, the bell in the tower is sounding. There is a whiff of incense in the air. The acolytes and choirs are forming the procession. The clergy in their multi-colored robes are patiently waiting for the organ prelude to conclude. I've reserved a special seat for you. The Church of Jesus Christ is gathering to offer *The Great Thanksgiving.* The words of Holy Scripture will be read, studied, and explained. Prayers, both ancient and modern, will be offered. The holy bread and wine will be shared. I'm so glad that you are here.

Thanks for reading,

Dennis Roy Maynard

Primary Character Review

Falls City, Georgia

This is a fictional town in South Georgia. It's just the kind of place most all of us would like to call home. If our ancestors were white Europeans, certain privileges belong to us. If we inherited their land and money, life would even be better. Many of the historic buildings and homes still stand along the tree-lined streets with manicured lawns.

Historic First Church (Episcopal)

It is the parish of the socially elite. This is the parish to join after you've been accepted into membership at the country club. Serving on the First Church Vestry is a plus for young attorneys seeking partnership in their law firms. The Church, regardless of denomination, plays a major role in the lives of the citizens of this community. The fact is that if you don't attend a church on Sunday, you'd better hide your car in the garage.

The Reverend and Mrs. Steele Austin

Steele and Randi are a most unlikely couple to be called as the rector and spouse of Historic First Church. Father Austin's understanding of the Gospel continually clashes with the unwritten membership standards of the parish. His inclusive mission is an affront to the way of life the current members and their ancestors fought to maintain. Still, as rector of one of the most prestigious congregations in Georgia, he wields tremendous influence in the affairs of the community and the state.

Almeda Alexander Drummond

She is the undisputed *grand dame* of First Church. Almeda is a powerbroker that few dare to cross. Her arrogant spirit finds its origin in the life of poverty she lived before marrying wealth. That same strong spirit led to her remarkable recovery from a debilitating stroke.

Chadsworth Purcell Alexander

His ancestors left him a fortune that he continues to further enrich. He was seduced into marrying Almeda after she and her mother managed to put him in a drunken stupor. He lived a double life in Falls City as a closeted gay man. When his secret was about to be discovered, he faked his suicide. He disappeared and took the identity of his dead lover, Earle LaFitte.

Doctor Horace Drummond

He is the African American priest called by Father Austin to be the senior associate at First Church. The widowed Almeda Alexander shocked the entire community by marrying him.

Mary Alice Smythe

She is the undisputed head of the politically powerful First Church Altar Guild. She has been president of the Guild for decades. No one dares challenge her for the position.

Stone Clemons

Stone is a wise attorney and counselor to Father Austin. He is one of Father Austin's strongest advocates and defenders.

Virginia Mudd Willoughby

She is one of the most dysfunctional personalities in Falls City. At one time she was a powerbroker at First Church. Her addiction to drugs and sex destroyed her marriage and reputation. Her complete lack of a superego ultimately landed her in prison. Her new attorney husband, Thackston Willoughby, managed her release and getting all charges against her expunged.

Chief Joe Sparks

He is known simply as *the Chief*. He's a close boyhood friend of Stone Clemons. He is the Falls City Chief of Police. Along with Stone, they are Steele's closest friends and defenders in the parish.

Mr. and Mrs. Henry Mudd

He is a leading attorney in Falls City, and a strong friend and supporter of the rector. Once he divorced Virginia and took custody of their two daughters, he married the beautiful Delilah. They are parenting two daughters from Henry's first marriage to Virginia. Their first child together mirrored the ancestry of Dee's biological father. He was Jamaican.

Howard and Martha Dexter

Howard is the keeper of the treasury at First Church. He is a constant critic of the rector's financial management of the parish. His own greed and stinginess leaves his wife, Martha, to resort to begging for food at every social occasion. Martha is Mary Alice Smythe's constant companion.

Colonel Mitchell

He's not a real Colonel. His first name is *Colonel.* He is a non-recovering alcoholic with incredible control needs. His dry drunk behavior is acted out frequently and maliciously. His envy and jealousy of Steele Austin's popularity and success keeps him seething.

Tom Barnhardt

It is commonly accepted that Tom, and the partners in his law firm, have made their fortune by stealing from the widows and orphans. Tom's only investment in First Church is separating the parish and the school. He believes the only way he can achieve his goal is to destroy the rector's integrity and credibility.

Elmer Idle

At one time he was married to Judith. Together they made one of the most disgustingly pious couples at First Church. Their fundamentalism caused them to continually clash with the rector. Ultimately they left the parish to unite with the fundamentalist Saint Andrew's Presbyterian Church. Soon after their arrival, Judith had an adulterous relationship with the senior pastor, Melvin MacClaren. They left their respective spouses, got Mexican divorces, and were married in Mexico.

The Right Reverend Sean Evans

Sean had always wanted to be a bishop. Now he is bishop of one of the most conservative dioceses in the Episcopal Church. He must keep his homosexuality a highly guarded secret. He and Rabbi Ezequiel Dolan have fallen in love with each other. They continue to hide their sexuality and their relationship from their respective congregations and other clergy.

Jim Vernon

At one time, Jim was in a committed same sex relationship with Bishop Sean Evans. Jim rejected Sean when the bishop gained too much weight. The rejection hurt Sean so deeply that he ended his relationship with Jim. In spite of that he retained Jim as his diocesan canon.

The Reverend Melvin MacClaren and his wife, Rose

Rose was the longsuffering wife of The Reverend Melvin MacClaren. In order to escape and cope with their abusive marriage, she learned how to grow marijuana plants. After her husband deserted her and their three children, Rose established a seamstress business with the assistance and guidance of Almeda Alexander Drummond.

The resemblance of any character in this novel to persons living or dead is not intended. However, since we all have a dark side, each of us will most likely see ourselves or another in one or more of the good citizens residing in Falls City, Georgia.

In spite of multiple reads and the excellent efforts of our editor, little punctuation and spelling gremlins seem to slip inside every book. For any little gremlins you discover in this one, we offer you our sincerest apologies and beg your understanding and forgiveness.

THE MESSY MAGNOLIA

BOOK NINE

EPILOGUE

"Father Austin, Thackston and I would like for you to come to lunch."

Steele hesitated. He still had reservations about Virginia Mudd Willoughby. "Where would you like me to meet you?"

"Oh, normally we'd take you to the club, but Thackston is working from home this week. He's got a challenging case about to go to trial. He agreed to work at home so that he could still make time for me. You do remember that was your suggestion?"

"No, I don't remember making that particular suggestion, but I'm glad that he's following through on making time for you."

"We'd also like to give you another check for your Habitat House."

"Gosh, you have already been so generous."

"Actually, Father, Thackston wants to see how much you've raised. He's considering giving you the balance of what you need."

Steele was silent.

"Hello. Are you still there?"

"I'm sorry. Yes, I'm still here. You said Thackston would be joining us for lunch?"

"Yes. He's working from home. Do you like *Monte Cristo* sandwiches?"

"I haven't eaten a *Monte Cristo* in years."

"Well, you are in for a treat. My housekeeper makes the best *Monte Cristo* sandwiches."

"So your housekeeper will be there too?"

"Why do you ask? She'll be making our lunch. I told her to keep it simple. Thackston will eat with us and then go back across the hall to his study to work. He'll want to get right to the point. So if you could have a total of what you need for the Habitat Project handy, that would help."

"Of course. When did you want me to come?"

"Thackston likes to break for his lunch at 11:30 sharp. Would that work for you?"

"When?"

Virginia giggled. "Could you come tomorrow?"

"Yes, tell Thackston, I'll see you tomorrow just before 11:30."

Virginia smiled as she thought about her conversation with Steele Austin the day before. She was dressed in a white blouse without a bra. She decided on a knee length black skirt. She was barefoot as she waited on Steele to arrive. Her housekeeper answered the door and showed Steele into the library.

Virginia greeted him with a smile and a handshake. "Thanks for coming to our home, Father Austin, I hope it's acceptable that we have lunch here in Thackston's library." Steele could see that a small table had been prepared with three place settings on it. His reservations about being alone with Virginia in her home began to dissipate.

"Oh, I'm sure this will be fine."

"Thackston will join us shortly. He's on the telephone with one of his clients. I had my housekeeper prepare some sweet tea. May I pour you a glass?"

"Thanks, that would be nice."

Virginia stood at the table and poured Steele a glass of sweet tea. She glanced out the window and saw her housekeeper walking down the driveway. She was on her way to the bus stop. Virginia had given her the rest of the day off. Thackston was up in Augusta playing in a charitable golf tournament. Everything was going according to her plan. Virginia reached into her blouse pocket and retrieved a small vial of GHB. She poured it into Steele's tea.

"Thanks." Steele swallowed some of the tea. "You said Thackston would be joining us."

"Yes, as I said, he's on the telephone in his study. He'll be right in. Please have a seat on the sofa. I need to go into the kitchen and see how my housekeeper is coming along with lunch. I'll also stop by Thackston's study and let him know you've arrived. Make yourself comfortable. I'll be right back."

Steele sat down and drank some more of his tea. He put his hand on his forehead. He was feeling a bit nauseous. His vision was blurry. Everything was getting foggy. When he heard Virginia return he tried to stand up. "Virginia, I'm afraid I'm having some vertigo. I really feel dizzy."

"Oh, are you sick?"

"I d-o-n't k-no-w..." Steele slurred his words.

"Why don't you lie down? I'll get you a cold cloth."

Virginia couldn't be happier. She'd gone up to Atlanta and visited a gay leather bar. She pretended to be a newspaper reporter doing an article on gay rape. She wanted to know if date rape drugs would work on men. She found the bartender was more than willing to talk. She thought he was pretty rough looking. He was dressed in leather and chains. He wasn't very attractive, so she figured that if anyone would need to use date rape drugs on a guy, it was that bartender.

Not only was he quite familiar with the various drugs, but he also let her know that he just happened to have them on hand for a price. He described the three most common date rape drugs. He admitted to preferring GHB. He told her that it worked best as a clear liquid that had no odor and was without taste. It was quick acting and left no trace in the blood stream. The target would be disoriented, dizzy, and mostly unaware of what was happening to them. He said the best part was that after a few hours, they would not be able to remember if they'd even had sex.

"Can men have sex on that drug?" Virginia asked.

"You may have to do some oral on them to get them engorged, but yes, they'll be able to function. They just won't remember doing it."

"Virginia, I d----on'---t..." Steele's words faded into a whisper.

Virginia unbuttoned Steele's shirt and ran her hands over his chest. "Nice," she smiled.

Steele tried to push her arms away, but his strength failed him. He wanted to lift his arms to push her off him, but he was paralyzed. He felt himself trying to shake his head, but his head wouldn't move. He was screaming for her to stop, but no sound was coming from his mouth. Steele's mind sank away in confusion and dizziness. His eyes were so blurry he could not clearly see his surroundings. He wanted to resist Virginia, but he could not get his body to cooperate. He felt himself losing consciousness.

"Now, now. You just lie there and relax." Virginia studied Steele's chest. She kissed his lips, his neck, and smothered his chest with even more kisses.

"Now, let's see just what you have to share with Virginia. I'm sure you're going to be able to make me very happy. We'll both be happy." Virginia ran her hands through the hair on his chest. "It's a shame you won't remember just how happy Virginia is going to make you."

She began unbuckling the belt on his pants. She glanced up at Steele's face. Clearly, the drug was working just as the bartender had told her. He was completely incapacitated. He had no idea as to what she was about to do to him. It didn't matter to Virginia. This was not about his pleasure. It was about hers.

A satisfied look washed over her face. "You're not going to remember this, Father Austin, but you will enjoy it." She tugged again at his belt, trying to release it from the buckle.

Suddenly, Virginia's body was jolted upright. A wave of panic washed over her. She was shocked by the sound of a familiar voice. Her husband was walking toward her. "Virginia, what the hell are you doing to that priest?"

The Magnolia Series

Dennis R. Maynard

Like a magnolia tree planted by a pure stream,
The roots of the faithful run deep.
The dew glistens on their dark green leaves.
The blossoms shine brilliantly in the morning sun.
A storm spreads their sweet perfume for all to enjoy.

THE LAST MAGNOLIA

BOOK TEN

1

"Our boy's in trouble!" Chief Sparks used his car phone to call Stone Clemons. "I'll be pulling up in front of your office in three minutes. Come on out. I'll pick you up."

"I'll be waiting."

"Light it up." The Chief instructed his driver to turn on the patrol car's lights and siren.

Stone Clemons was standing at the curb when they arrived at his office. He sat in the back seat. "What's going on?"

"I really don't know. One of my officers telephoned me. He'd received an emergency summons to the residence of Thackston Willoughby. EMS is on the scene. He said he recognized the man they were treating as Father Austin. He knew he was my priest so he notified me."

Stone grimaced and shut his eyes. "I don't have a good feeling about this."

Within minutes they pulled up in front of the Willoughby house. The EMS ambulance, a fire truck, and another squad car were in the driveway. Stone asked, "What's the fire truck doing here?"

"When possible we dispatch the fire department. They often have life saving equipment that the EMS personnel might not have with them."

As they entered the house the firemen were leaving. The Chief asked, "You guys weren't needed?"

"No, EMS has everything under control."

When Chief Sparks and Stone walked into the living room they saw the EMS personnel lifting a shirtless Steele Austin onto a gurney. "What's wrong with him?"

"We really don't know. We're transporting him to the emergency room. His heart rate, breathing, blood pressure, and temperature are all below normal. When he tries to speak he slurs his words. There are multiple possibilities. He comes in and out of consciousness. We need the ER Doctors to figure it out."

Stone took Steele's hand. "Padre, the Chief and I are here. Can you understand what I'm saying?"

Steele's eyes widened. He tried to speak but his words did not make sense.

"Hang in there. These fellows are going to take you to the hospital." Stone studied Steele's bare chest, arms, and hands. "The Chief and I will be over in a few minutes." With that the EMS attendants moved Steele to the ambulance.

The Chief had been watching Thackston and Virginia. They were leaning up against the wall near the fireplace. Thackston had his arms wrapped around Virginia. She was visibly upset as tears were streaming down her face. "Mister Willoughby, what happened here?"

"The only thing I know is that when I came home Father Austin was passed out on our couch. Virginia was trying to give him CPR. She thought he'd had a heart attack. I took his pulse. It felt fine to me so I didn't think he'd had a heart attack, but perhaps he'd had a stroke. I dialed 911. You all know the rest."

"What was he doing here?"

Virginia clung to her husband's arms. Her voice quivered and rose in pitch as she sounded more like a frightened little girl than a mature woman. "I invited him to come here for lunch with our housekeeper and me. Bernice wanted to talk with him about her church helping with the Habitat House we are helping to fund at First Church."

"Where's Bernice now?"

"She got a call from the school. One of her children is sick so she had to go pick him up."

The table with three place settings on it caught Stone's eye. "So you never got to eat your lunch?"

"No, we didn't get that far. Bernice let Father Austin in and brought him out here to the library. She poured him a glass of sweet tea. And then she got the phone call. He'd just barely arrived when she had to leave."

"Go on."

"Well, I was still getting ready when he arrived. But when I came out here I found him lying on our couch. He was clutching his chest. I was just certain he was having a heart attack. That's when I opened his shirt. I began doing CPR on him like I'd seen people do on television."

"Did you check to see if he had a pulse before doing CPR on him?"

"No, I didn't think of that. I was just so shocked. I guess I panicked. Thank God Thackston arrived when he did." Virginia began to cry again. Through her sobs she uttered, "I just don't know what I would've done. I do pray that Father Austin will be all right."

Stone tapped the Chief on the arm and gave him a nod that they needed to leave. The Chief nodded in return. When they were in the patrol car Stone spoke first. "I smell a rat."

The Chief agreed. "Her story is just not adding up."

"When we get over to the hospital I want you to instruct them to do a complete workup on him. I think you should also have them do a rape kit."

The Chief shot Stone a surprised look. "What? Have you actually become that jaundiced in your old age? Do you really think that woman was trying to rape him?"

"Did you see the lipstick marks on Steele?"

"No, I didn't look that closely."

"Well, the last time I checked you don't need to leave lipstick on a body to do CPR."

"You just may have missed your calling. You've wasted all these years practicing law when you could have been in law enforcement."

"Well, I do have one more thing I want to give you." Stone reached into his jacket pocket. "I want your lab to check this."

"You sly dog. But first things first, we need to swing by and pick up Steele's wife and take her with us to the hospital."

The Magnolia Series

Dennis R. Maynard

CHAPTER

2

"What are you doing?"

Rose MacClaren smiled, "I was thinking about you."

"That's nice." Elmer Idle felt a warm glow wash over his body. "That's why I phoned you. I haven't been able to get you out of my mind since last night."

"It was wonderful. I never dreamed that being intimate with a man could be so... so... I don't know how to describe it. I just know how it felt to be with you last night."

"No guilt?"

"A little. I stared at myself in the mirror this morning. I kept asking, 'Rose MacClaren, just who are you? Here you are unmarried and having sex. This is no way for a pastor's wife to behave, even if you are the ex-wife of a pastor.' "

"Well, did you get an answer?"

"No, I just decided that if God is going to send me to hell because I'm fornicating with the man I love, then it's going to be worth it."

Elmer chuckled, "I guess we'll be in hell together."

"But, Honey, how can something that feels so heavenly be sinful enough to damn you to the eternal fires?"

"Well, it's a moot point anyway because soon we'll be husband and wife."

"Has Father Austin heard back from the bishop?"

"Not yet. He said it could take a month or so, but he didn't think it would be a problem. We were both victims of adulterous spouses, so the bishop should be willing to grant us permission to be married in the Church. I'm really not that worried about it."

"It was kind of embarrassing filling out those forms for the bishop."

"I know. We have no reason to be ashamed. I was married to a controlling religious nut. And you were married to an abusive husband. It's just pure Karma that they ended up having an affair with each other and getting married."

"You know what I think?"

"No, tell me. I don't think it was Karma that led you into my shop that day. I think God brought you to me."

"I think so too and I'm so happy." Elmer paused. "You know how you were describing our love life?"

"Yes."

"It's the same for me. I know you don't want to hear this but sex with Judith was more like a duty. I just wanted to get it over with."

Rose snickered, "It couldn't have been all that bad."

"Oh, don't get me wrong. I don't lie to myself. I got my release out of it, but that was about all there was to it."

"Well, at least you got that. I did get my three beautiful children, but other than that, nothing."

"Have you talked to Almeda?"

"Elmer, she's taking over our wedding reception. She insists that we have it at her mansion. She wants to plan every detail."

"Is she letting you have any input?"

"She listens to my ideas. Smiles. Pats my hand and reassures me that it's going to be a wonderful reception."

"Have you given her any names for the guest list?"

"I don't have many names. Just a few of my customers that are regulars and some of the people I've met at church. How about you?"

"I'm afraid that I'm in the same boat. I lost a lot of my close friends at First Church. When I followed Judith's lead and turned on Father Austin, people turned against us. It was the final straw for some when we went over to your husband's former church. Even more folks cut us out of their lives."

"Well, I don't guess we have to worry. Almeda insists that she's going to make sure that all the right people show up for our reception."

"You do know who she's talking about?"

"*The Country Club Set*, I guess."

Elmer chuckled again, "*The Country Club Set* would not be good enough. She's going for *The Magnolia Club Muckety-Mucks.*"

"At least she's not trying to plan our wedding service in the chapel. Are you still okay with that?"

"Of course I am. An intimate wedding in the chapel is perfect. Have you chosen your dress?"

"Not yet. I really felt strange about wearing white. I mean, I thought you could only do that at your first wedding, but Almeda says otherwise."

"What did she tell you?"

"She asked her husband, Father Drummond, to explain it to me."

"And?"

"It seems that a white wedding dress is actually a continuation of your baptismal gown. He explained that we are baptized in white gowns, received our first communion in white, are confirmed in white, priests are ordained in white, and when we die our casket is covered with a white cloth."

"It's called a pall."

"What is?"

"The white cloth that covers a casket. It's called a pall."

Rose let out a deep breath. "I guess in time I'll learn to speak Episcopalian."

"So you're okay wearing a white wedding dress?"

"I am now since Father Drummond explained it to me. I don't think any other color would make sense for a baptized Christian."

"I guess I'd better let you get back to work. There's a baseball game coming on the television that I want to watch." Elmer glanced at his television. He gasped. "Oh, my God. I don't believe it."

"Elmer, what's wrong?"

"Rose are you near a television?"

"There's one in my office."

"Hurry. Turn to Channel Four as fast as you can."

Rose ran to her office carrying her mobile phone. "What

is it, Elmer? What do you see? Okay, I'm turning to Channel Four." There was silence and then Rose screeched. "What are they doing here?"

They stood frozen staring at their respective televisions. The faces of their former spouses were plastered across the screens. They were standing in front of the Falls City Sports Arena. The banner flashing on the screen read, *"A Spiritual Revival Is Coming to Falls City this Sunday night . Join Judith MacClaren and The Reverend Melvin MacClaren to receive the blessing God has reserved just for you!"*

The Magnolia Series

Dennis R. Maynard

CHAPTER

3

Colonel Mitchell had been seething for weeks. He was so angry he'd not been able to eat or sleep. Having been trained in the ways of a strong Southern gentleman, he dealt with his pain the way any real man would. He restricted his calorie intake to healthy swigs of *Jim Beam*. That was his *go-to* for pain relief and nourishment. When he just needed quantity more than quality he would purchase a case of *Wild Turkey*. That served his purposes just fine. He never messed with the designer brands and award winners. They were too expensive. His taste buds weren't that refined.

Colonel knew what he wanted. Tom Barnhardt had been his greatest hope. They'd worked together to get rid of that recalcitrant priest. Every time he even thought about that so-called clergyman he could feel his blood boil. He literally believed his head was going to explode at the very sight of him. Barnhardt had agreed to help him get the goods on Steele Austin. But suddenly he'd turned on him. He wouldn't take his telephone calls. He'd even gone over to his office but Tom had refused to see him.

Colonel Mitchell was sitting at the gentlemen's bar in The Magnolia Club. No women were allowed in this part of the building. It was a place a man could go to shoot the breeze with his buddies or just sit and think. He could do so without having a gaggle of women disturb his peace with their incessant chatter. Colonel knew that damn Stone Clemons and his gun-toting sidekick Sparks had something to do with it all. Somehow or another they'd gotten to Tom and convinced him not to take down the rector. But how? What did they say to him? Or better yet, just what kind of deal did they make with him? He needed to find out.

Day after day for the past week he'd come to the club and taken a seat at the bar. He knew that Tom was in the habit of stopping here after work before going home. He'd missed him the last few days. He figured that he'd been out of town. So he telephoned Tom's office this morning. He asked his secretary if Mister Barnhardt was in town. She confirmed that he was. He hung up. Now he waited. He knew that today would be the day he could get some answers.

Sure enough, just as he turned on his seat to glance at the door, in walked Tom Barnhardt. He was dressed in his five thousand dollar suit and wearing his gold Omega watch. Colonel mused, that idiot thinks he's *James Bond*. He caught Tom's eye. He motioned for Tom to come sit next to him, but Tom ignored him. Colonel stood. He walked to where Tom was standing. He grabbed Tom's arm. "We used to be friends. We shared a common goal. I need to know what happened."

Tom shot him an angry look. "Are you drunk?"

"My friend, *Jim Beam,* has been keeping me company. For God's sake, we're in a bar."

Tom removed Colonel's hand from his arm. "I really don't have anything to discuss with you."

Colonel Mitchell felt tears welling up in his eyes. "I'm just trying to understand."

Tom stared at the pathetic excuse of a man standing before him. "Okay, I'll give you five minutes, but if you make a scene I'll have your sorry ass tossed out of this club."

"And just how do you plan on doing that? I've been a member of this club longer than you have."

Tom snickered. "I guess you haven't heard. I was just elected to a three-year term as President and Board Chairman of this club. Now go sit down in that booth over there and I'll be with you in a minute."

Tom walked to the bar and ordered. "Henry, my usual."

"Yes, suh, Mistuh Barnhardt. I'sa bring it to you over at the table if you's want."

"That'll be fine. Thanks."

"Okay, Mitchell, you have five minutes."

Colonel slurred his words as he asked the question that

had been haunting him, "Tom, what changed your mind? Why won't you help me get rid of that poor excuse for a rector?"

"I don't need to get rid of him. I can get my way without getting rid of him."

"What do you mean?" Colonel Mitchell waved for Henry to bring him another drink.

Tom stopped Henry with a nod and simple wave of his hand. "You've had enough. You're drunk. You don't need to be driving a car in the condition that you're in."

"I can handle my liquor. You just make sure you can handle yours."

"I'm telling you that if I see you get behind the wheel I'll call the police and have them pick you up."

"What's it to you?"

"I don't want you killing innocent people."

"You still haven't answered my question."

"Look, Mitchell, I told you from the beginning that I really don't care for Austin, but he's not my primary concern. The independence of the school has been my primary goal. I thought it was Austin that was standing in my way. I've since learned that he's not the problem."

"Oh, then who is?"

"It's all church politics. We just need a couple of well-placed funerals. Once those have occurred, Stone Clemons, Chief Sparks, and Father Austin will lead the movement to separate the school."

"So that's the deal you made."

"Well, actually it's more than that. I've gotten to know the rector. He's really not a bad guy if you give him a chance."

"What the hell has happened to you, Tom? The next thing you're going to tell me is that you're going to write him a fat check."

"I already have."

"You've what?"

"I wrote a fifty thousand dollar check to First Church and another fifty thousand dollar check to First Church School. But that's not the least of it. I'm thinking about running to be

Steele's senior warden at the annual meeting of the church."

"So now you call him Steele. If that doesn't beat all."

"Your five minutes are up. I'm going to have Henry call you a taxi. And Colonel, I don't think you and I have a single thing in common. There is no reason for us to converse about anything again. Do I make myself clear?"

Colonel Mitchell stood. "And you, sir, can pay my bar bill. And once you've done that you can go straight to hell."

Colonel Mitchell stumbled to the front steps of the club where a taxi was waiting on him. He got in and gave the driver his home address. He stared out the window at the passing buildings. Then something got his attention. He realized that his route home took him past multiple churches. There were Presbyterian, Lutheran, Methodist, Congregationalists, and others. Colonel Mitchell smiled. An idea that would keep him awake again tonight was beginning to take form in his mind.

The Magnolia Series

Dennis R. Maynard

CHAPTER

4

Father Jim Vernon's emotions had alternated between explosive anger and bouts of tear-filled sadness. He simply could not believe that Sean Evans had thrown him over for that muscle-bound rabbi.

Jim seethed as he recalled that Sean wouldn't even be a bishop if it weren't for his cleverness. He was the one that had rigged the election so that he could win. He reasoned that no good deed goes unpunished. In addition to that, they'd been lovers for years. They'd kept one another's mutual secret so they could remain in the priesthood. Just thinking about it all made him even angrier.

Jim had tried to get even with Sean and his *boy-toy* by exposing their relationship to a leading priest and lay member in the diocese, but that actually backfired on him. It also cost him his job. Sean fired him. That put him in a real dilemma. Just what is an unemployed and discredited priest supposed to do? Where is he supposed to go to find a new position?

He decided to return to what he'd done to help pay for his college and theological school. He'd wait tables in an upscale restaurant. He could have stayed in Savannah, but the thought of running into Sean and his man whore was just too much for him. He made the decision to move to Atlanta. It didn't take him long to find a job at a high-end steak house. As sad as it was, he knew he could make more money waiting tables than he could as a priest in a parish.

Even as his life settled into a routine, Jim felt the need to get even with Sean. He tried to do so the only way he knew how. He would have sex with as many men as he possibly could. He reasoned that not only would he be getting even with Sean, he would also be proving he was still irresistible. He wanted to prove to himself that he could have any man he wanted.

One of the other waiters had taken him to a private club for gay and bisexual men. It was very luxurious and located in an immaculate building with beautiful furnishings. There were several small private rooms for intimate relations discreetly placed around the central social room. This exclusive club was by membership only. No alcohol or drugs were allowed on the premises. If any member arrived intoxicated, a very large bouncer would turn them away. The only downside to membership in the club was you had to give them a copy of your driver's license. Jim's license photo showed him wearing a clerical collar. He needed to get a new license and photo before joining the club. Once he'd presented his new license, he quickly discovered the opportunities with some gorgeous men were unlimited. The club was only open from 10:00 p.m. to 5:00 a.m. so he could conveniently drop by after his shift at the restaurant.

Jim didn't limit his conquests to the club. Having sex with multiple partners each night had still left him with a hole in his heart. There was a fitness gym near his new apartment that catered to gay men. The whirlpool and steam room were meeting places for a quick hookup.

A few of the men he encountered wanted more than he was willing to give. They hoped to enter dating relationships. They needed to see if maybe something more permanent was in their future. That was not what Jim lusted after. He was keeping score. Each day on the wall calendar in his bedroom he recorded the type of sex he'd had and how many times. He mused that one day he'd take the calendar and shove it in Sean Evans' face. That would prove to him that he'd made a huge mistake. He'd dumped one of the most desirable men in the world for a rabbi. The very thought of that confrontation brought a smile to Jim's face.

There were no empty tables on Valentine's Day. The steak restaurant was packed for dinner. Reservations had closed the week before. Jim was especially pleased that there was a fixed menu that included surf and turf, baked potato, and a side salad. He would only have to take drink orders and ask, 'How would you like your steak cooked?' It could prove to be a hassle-free night. There would be no need for him to try to be patient while diners scanned the menu for the tenth time. He hated answering their multiple questions. There were times he just wanted to shout *Order something damn it. Make up your mind.* The best part of the evening for him was that his tips would not be shortchanged. In addition to the fixed price menu, a twenty percent gratuity would be automatically added to each check.

The evening seemed like it was flying by. Jim looked at his watch. Time for the nine o'clock reservations to be seated was approaching. He watched the tuxedoed maitre d' escort several couples to his station area. Two more hours and he could go over to the club. Then he spotted them. They were being led to one of the other rooms in the restaurant. At first he thought his eyes might be deceiving him. No, he was right the first time. Strutting across the floor into an adjacent room were the two people he despised most in life.

In the kitchen he asked the manager, "Who's working the garden room?"

"Sylvia."

"Which one is she?" Jim had not bothered to get to know the names of all his fellow employees. However, there was one busboy that smiled at him in a flirtatious manner. He did ask him for his name and phone number.

"She's the loud redhead. We only hired her for tonight. She used to work here on a regular basis. Now she just fills in when we need her."

Jim waited on her to come back to the kitchen. "There are two forty-something men at one of your tables."

"I'll say. They are knockouts, but I think they might be gay."

"What makes you think so?"

"Duh. They're holding hands and looking at each other all googly-eyed."

"Well, actually they're friends of mine. And yes, they are gay. Would you mind if I served them? I don't want your

38

tip. I just want to be able to take them their food and talk with them a bit."

"If you're anxious to do my work for me, have at it. Just remember, the money is mine."

"Deal."

"Their salads are up and ready to go."

Jim picked up the two salads and walked into the pantry. He shut the pantry door behind him. He took a bottle of *Tabasco* off the shelf. Shoved some of the lettuce aside and applied it liberally. He covered the *Tabasco* with more lettuce. He looked around to make sure no one was watching him. He spit on both of the salads and stirred his saliva into the dressing.

Sean recognized him first. Jim was approaching their table. He had a big smile on his face. "Happy Valentine's Day, guys. When I saw you enter I just knew that I had to be the one to bring your dinner to you." He placed their salads before each of them. He leaned over so that his face was directly between theirs. In a husky voice he whispered so only they could hear, "Eat your salads, Mattress Munchers. And have a Happy V Day." Jim then turned and walked away.

The Magnolia Series

Dennis R. Maynard

5

"Virginia, what happened here?"

"I told you, Thackston, I thought the man was having a heart attack."

"No, please start from the beginning. Tell me again why Father Austin was here." Thackston Willoughby loved Virginia with all his heart. He believed she was his soulmate.

From time to time he still had pangs of guilt about the adulterous affair that he'd had with her. His love for Virginia had cost him his marriage, tied his name to a public scandal, and even a criminal investigation. He'd lost a few clients in his law practice because of her. He realized that he had now joined the ranks of men that have made a major sacrifice for the love of a woman. He so desperately wanted to believe that this entire event was exactly as she had described it.

His instincts, training, and experience as an attorney were gnawing at him. There were other times that he had suspicions Virginia was lying to him, but they were so minor he never challenged her. And then there were the occasions he knew for a fact she was lying to him. He'd let them slide as well.

He also knew she was a flirt. When he caught her he was amused by her immaturity. He dismissed her flirtations with other men as a harmless attempt to overcome some misplaced insecurity. He reasoned that she needed to flirt to compensate for her feelings of inferiority around other women. However, this time it was different. He wasn't going to be able to let go of the questions haunting him around this event.

"It's like I told you and the police, I invited Father Austin over here to meet with our maid, Bernice. I had told her about the Habitat House we are helping to fund. She thought her church would want to participate in the project." Virginia was confident she could get Bernice to agree to her story. If she refused, she would threaten her to within an inch of her life. Bernice was already afraid of Virginia, so she was confident that she would not cross her.

"Why didn't her pastor come to the meeting? If his church is going to put up half the money, then it looks like he would want to be in on the decision."

Virginia answered indignantly, "Thackston, I don't know. You'll just have to ask her. I never said that they were going to put up the other half of the money. Maybe Bernice wanted to gather all the details from Father Austin and then tell her pastor about the project. I can't read minds. I was simply trying to do her a favor. After all, she has been an excellent maid for us."

"So you were going to sit down with both of them over lunch?"

"Well, yes. Look at the table over there. I had her make provisions for the three of us. There are three place settings on the table."

That answer just didn't ring true for Thackston. If there was ever a social snob in Falls City it was his wife. Not only was she a social snob, he also knew her true feelings about African Americans. He didn't want to think of her as a racist even though he knew she thought of herself as their superior. "Okay, Virginia, I've got to ask. When did you decide it was acceptable to sit down at the same meal table with our maid?"

Virginia tried to keep her face from expressing the panic boiling up in her stomach. "Thackston, I don't understand why you are asking me all these questions. Honey, are you cross-examining me? Are you accusing me of some misbehavior? I love you. I would never lie to you or betray you."

A twinge of guilt quickened his conscience. He knew she loved him. But something just wasn't right. "I know you love me. You're going to have to excuse me. I'm an attorney. I need to have the events clear in my own mind. You know the people in this town. Someone is bound to ask me about all this."

"Who would be questioning you?" Virginia resorted to

one of her tried and true methods. She put Thackston on the defensive. She'd done it multiple times with her first husband, Henry Mudd. She knew if she could only get him to feel guilty about being suspicious then he would cease and desist.

Thackston wasn't playing. "Virginia, I have a hard time seeing you sitting at the same table and sharing a meal with our *Help*."

Virginia forced a tear to roll down her cheek. Over the years she'd perfected the technique. She could effortlessly squeeze out a tear when it was needed to serve her purpose. "Thackston, I'm really hurt. I feel like you don't believe me. I think you're accusing me of something. I just don't know what it is."

Thackston put his arms around her and brought her close. "Honey, please stop crying. I'm not accusing you of anything. Like I said, I want to have the series of events and facts fresh in my mind."

"Why, Thackston? Why is that so important?"

"Virginia, there's going to be gossip. This entire affair is going to be the talk of the town for weeks. I need to be able to respond."

A chill ran up her spine when he referred to the event as an affair. She needed to distract him. Virginia wiped the tears from her cheeks and pulled away from his embrace. "Okay, please ask me anything you want."

"Just one more thing. What made you think you needed to open Father Austin's shirt?"

"Isn't that what you do when you give CPR? I don't know. I thought that's what you do. I mean, that's what they do on television. I was just doing what I'd seen them do on those medical shows."

"But you don't know how to do CPR."

"I don't even know how to take a pulse. But after this event, I think both of us should take one of those courses they offer at the hospital. Don't you?"

"That sounds like a good idea."

"Do you have any more questions?"

"No, not right now, but if I think of something may I ask without you suspecting that I'm accusing you of not telling me the truth?"

"Thackston, I love you. I have never lied to you about anything and I never will."

The realization that she'd lied to him in the past washed over him. As an attorney he knew that people were as sinful as the options they had before them. For now, he'd accept her story as she'd told it, but he was going to talk to Bernice.

Virginia put her arms around Thackston's neck. She gave him a passionate kiss. After their embrace, Thackston retired to his study. Virginia began taking the dishes and silver from the table in the library back to the kitchen. Then she remembered the glass that she'd given to Steele. She returned to the library to look for it. Panic rose up in her chest. It was nowhere to be found.

The Magnolia Series

Dennis R. Maynard

6

The speed at which cell phone signals bounce off the satellites circling the planet is pathetic in comparison to the speed with which gossip can spread through Falls City. This is especially true for those that live inside the tiny kingdom occupied by the city's most elite citizens. This expensive and exclusive living space has three primary landmarks within its triangle. They are the all-male Magnolia Club, the Falls City Country Club, and First Church (Episcopal). When the rector of First Church is the topic of gossip, the speed at which it is transmitted exceeds the speed of light. It is for this reason alone that The Reverend Doctor Horace Drummond was not surprised to hear himself being paged at Falls City Hospital. Likewise, he was quite certain of the voice he would hear at the other end of the telephone line.

"This is Doctor Drummond."

"Horace, I am so angry with you right now. Why didn't you call me as soon as you were informed? You know just how much I love Steele and Randi."

"Almeda, Honey, I just arrived. I'm still trying to gather all the details."

"I heard that Steele had a heart attack."

"No, they've ruled out a heart attack."

"Then what's wrong with him?"

"The doctor is still evaluating the situation."

"Is Steele conscious?"

"Yes, when I got here he was sitting up in the bed. There was a nurse in there with Randi and him. She's talking with him about something. She asked everyone to step out of the room. She wanted to talk to just the two of them."

"So he's all right?"

"Like I said, he's sitting up and talking."

"You said the nurse asked everyone to step out. Who

else is there?"

"Chief Sparks and Stone Clemons are both here. They picked Randi up and brought her over."

"Who's staying with Randi's children?"

"I don't know. I'll ask Stone when I go back down there. I'm sure she didn't leave them alone."

"Never mind. I'll drive over to their house and check on them myself."

"I think I should go back and see if the nurse has left the room. I want to pray with Steele."

"No, wait. Is it true?"

"Is what true?"

"I heard that this happened when Steele was over at that awful Mudd woman's house."

"You mean Virginia Willoughby?"

"You know exactly who I mean. Was he there?"

I believe that's correct."

"Horace, I told you about her. When it comes to men she is worse than a pariah. I can't believe Steele would be alone with her in her house."

"He wasn't."

"He wasn't what?"

"He wasn't alone with her. My understanding is that both her husband and their maid were supposed to be there."

"Hmm. Horace, I don't trust her."

"As you've told me multiple times. Almeda, I really think I should go back down there. I'll find out what I can and call you later."

"Okay, just make sure you do. I want to be your first phone call. The gossips in this town are having a field day. I need to be able to put a stop to some of the awful things that are being said about our rector."

"Like what?"

"Oh Horace, you wouldn't believe some of the stories making the rounds. Some are pure fancy. The only people that would believe them are the ones that have already made up their minds that they don't like Steele. Just call me when you've gathered the facts."

"You will be my first call."

When Horace returned to the examination room all the curtains were drawn. A tearful Randi and Chief Sparks were standing outside. Horace glanced under the exam room curtains and could see Steele's bare legs and feet standing on a large white sheet of paper. He heard Stone's voice as he conversed with Steele and the nurse. He wrinkled his brow. At first he was confused. He heard the nurse giving Steele disrobing instructions. It was then that he understood exactly what was happening. He asked Chief Sparks to confirm his suspicion.

The Chief nodded.

The Magnolia Series

Dennis R. Maynard

7

As soon as the nurse opened the curtains to reveal Steele Austin lying on the exam room bed, Randi hurried to his side. He was wearing a hospital gown. The nurse and Stone walked directly to Chief Sparks. She handed him a large brown bag with a seal on it. "This is his *SAEK*. I'll need you to sign for it."

The Chief nodded, "Okay, but first I want to make sure everything is being done by the book. I need to ask you some questions. Are you a licensed *SANE*?"

"I am."

"Is your license current?"

"Yes, I've held my license for ten years now. And I take all the continuing education courses before each renewal."

"Where did you get your *SANE Degree*?"

"From Cleveland University. It was actually one of the pioneers in this forensic science."

"Mister Clemons, you served as Steele's advocate. Did Father Austin freely consent to each aspect of the exam?"

"He did."

"Was any part of the exam not conducted?"

Stone lowered his voice so that Randi could not hear him. "He did not want to do the anal swab or probe. I agreed that it was most likely unnecessary."

"Okay, duly noted."

Chief Sparks took the brown bag from the nurse and signed for it. "Can we take him home?"

"You'll need to discuss that with his doctor. He has ordered an IV. Father Austin appears to be dehydrated. He's not signed the order yet, but I think he wants to keep him here overnight for observation."

As the nurse was walking away Horace whispered to Chief Sparks, "I've got to ask some questions."

"Let's step over there to the waiting area. I don't want to upset Randi any more than she already is."

"Okay, Preacher, shoot."

"First, you were using some acronyms with that nurse I've never heard before. What do they mean?"

"She's a *SANE*. That stands for *Sexual Assault Nurse Examiner*. She's a highly specialized and licensed forensic examiner. Not every hospital has one. We're fortunate that they do here."

Horace grimaced, "Well, that confirms my suspicions. I thought that was what she was doing in there. And the *SAEK* bag she gave you, what is that? No wait, I think I'm smart enough to get that one. Does it stand for *Sexual Assault Exam Kit*?"

"You can now go to the head of the class."

"Why do you believe all of that is necessary?"

"Let's get Stone over here. We were simply responding to one of his hunches."

Just then Stone walked up. "They're going to keep him here overnight. Randi wants us to swing by her house and get Steele some pajamas. She told me where to look. She wants to stay with him until he gets settled in a room."

Chief Sparks nodded. "One of my female officers is at their house with the children. We can call and have her bring the pajamas over. I got a call from her a few minutes ago. She said Almeda was there with the children so she wasn't needed."

"That works for me."

"Let's find a room where we can talk."

Horace volunteered to lead them to one of the private family rooms surrounding the hospital chaplain's office. Once they were seated Chief Sparks began, "Tell us, Stone, what do you think they found?"

"After Steele was completely undressed the *SANE* used an ultraviolet light on him. It showed traces of saliva in some mighty strange places. She swabbed those areas."

"So that confirmed your earlier suspicions?"

Stone smiled. "I have to confess it was a lucky guess. The lipstick I spotted on him was ever so light. It could have been most anything, but there was just enough there to pique my curiosity. Virginia has quite the reputation in this town."

Horace interrupted, "I find it hard to believe she would have tried anything like that with her husband there."

Stone shook his head, "Her husband wasn't there the entire time. He arrived home to find her supposedly giving Steele CPR. He's the one that called EMS."

Horace sat back in his seat and slapped his forehead. "Oh my God, this entire mess could end up being a major scandal. Almeda called and told me the gossips have already run amuck."

"So did the *SANE* take blood and urine samples?"

"Yes, it took a little while for Steele to become coherent enough to give his consent to each aspect of the exam. Chief, I'm telling you he was drugged. I think the lab tests will prove it. How long will that take?"

"If it was what I suspect it was, it's going to take a few days. We're not equipped to test all the drugs that are out there on the market. I'm going to send the samples up to the forensics lab in Atlanta. If the tests are negative, we'll get an answer in a couple of days. If the samples end up being positive, the results could take three or four days. Did you see or hear anything else during the exam that you think I need to know?"

"Steele has no memory of anything happening. The only thing he can completely recall is ringing their doorbell. He was supposed to have lunch with Virginia and her husband to talk about the Habitat House. He does remember that much. Beyond that he can't recall a thing. His first memory is seeing Randi holding his hand here in the hospital."

"So Steele was under the impression that he was having lunch with both of them?" The Chief wanted to double-check his facts.

"Now you're catching on. The city just might be able to get her money's worth if you keep doing your job." Stone and

Chief Sparks enjoyed teasing each other.

"You and I both know I'm overworked and underpaid."

Horace shook his head, "Okay, you guys sound like you're on top of getting to the bottom of this, but right now we need a story. What are we going to tell folks?"

Stone twisted his mouth and then pointed his finger at the Chief. "You tell me if this would have a negative impact on any charges you might bring in the future. I think we go with the story as Steele understood it. He went over to their house to have lunch with both of the Willoughbys. They were going to talk about the Habitat Project. All was going well until he felt ill and passed out. The doctors ran some tests and are keeping him in the hospital overnight. Beyond that there is no story. What do you think?"

Chief Sparks agreed. "Sounds like as good a story as any. If we bring charges, they'll be based on the evidence and not gossip. What do you think, Doctor Drummond?"

"After what I've learned here this afternoon, I think our first job is to protect Steele, Randi, and the people at First Church. We have a story. Let's stick to it until the evidence comes in. Now if you gentlemen will excuse me, I'm going to find Steele. I want to pray with him."

The Magnolia Series

Dennis R. Maynard

CHAPTER

8

"Is he wearing makeup?" Rose had been staring at her office television in disbelief. Elmer was doing the same in his condo. The faces of their ex spouses, who had cheated on them with each other and were now married, were on the local station.

"Maybe he's got a tan." Elmer answered.

"No, I don't think so. His face has always had a rugged reddish tone. He's definitely wearing makeup."

"That suit he's wearing didn't come off the discount rack at Macy's. That's one high dollar piece of cloth."

"And what do you think of her?"

"It looks to me she's gone pretty heavy on the makeup as well. Is she wearing false eyelashes?"

"I've never worn a pair, but they don't look real to me. I can also tell you that dress she's wearing cost a pretty penny. And I don't know who did her hair, but I want their number."

"Give me a second, I need to turn the volume up on my television. I want to hear what they're saying."

"Me too." Rose and Elmer remained on the telephone with each other.

"Ladies and Gentlemen of Falls City and surrounding communities. I know many of you will remember me when I was the senior pastor at Saint Andrew's Presbyterian Church. The beautiful woman standing next to me is my wife, Judith. It was no less than the hand of God that brought us together when we were victims of a terrible storm that ravaged each of our lives. That storm was no fault of either one of us, but our Great God in His providence brought us together." The Reverend Melvin MacClaren and Judith then looked at each other adoringly before returning their faces to the camera.

"Yes, and praise Jesus our wonderful God led us into an exciting ministry that has been prospering throughout the country of Mexico." Judith smiled sweetly. "And now we are so excited to share this blessing with all of you."

Melvin raised his voice. "GOD WANTS TO GIVE EACH OF YOU A VERY SPECIAL BLESSING!"

Judith nodded, "Yes, Jesus." In a voice that literally dripped with honey she continued. "God does not want you to be living paycheck to paycheck. He does not want you to spend your life worrying about how you are going to provide for your family. The Lord Jesus came so we might have life and have it more abundantly. He said nothing about just existing to survive day by day."

"When my wife, Judith, and I moved to Mexico to begin a new ministry, we literally had nothing but the clothes on our backs. But God has blessed us. We started our church in a meeting room in one of the hotels. Now look at what the Lord has done." Several photos of a large church's exterior and interior rotated on the screen. "Our beautiful sanctuary seats over five thousand people every Sunday. It's situated on a fifty acre campus with a school and a university center for training others in ministry."

Judith continued, "But God has not just blessed our ministry. He told us that He wanted to bless us personally. So God told us to build a beautiful home in which to reside." Photos of a very large house with a huge swimming pool, a tennis court, and a golf putting green surrounded by a large fence lingered on the screen.

"Brothers and sisters," Elmer crooned smoothly, "God has blessed us so we can bless you. We are here to tell you exactly how the Savior wants to bless each of you. This Sunday night right here in the Falls City Sports Arena, you will hear God's plan for your life. You will learn the five steps needed to claim the wonderful blessings that God wants to give you."

Judith shook her head. "It really is so very sad. Pastor MacClaren and I did not comprehend all the riches that God wanted to give us. They were there all along. The only thing we needed to do was to reach out and claim that which was already ours.   We had to learn how to claim all these blessings. Now we want to teach you how to do the same."

"We could have stayed in Mexico in the comfort of our home and simply enjoyed the lifestyle God has afforded us." Melvin paused.

Judith continued, "But God laid a heavy burden on our hearts. He told us we must teach others how to accept the wondrous life He has planned for them. In particular, He told us we needed to return to this community."

"My friends, do you know that God has a wonderful plan for each of you? He knows each of you by name and He has a plan that corresponds with that name. No matter what your situation right now, it is not the plan God has for you. If you are unemployed or in a dead-end job, that's not in His plan. Are you lonely and have no one in your life to love? God has already chosen a loving man or woman to care for you. Are you burdened with debt? That's not God's plan for you either. And if you are ill and suffering pain or disability," Elmer paused again and looked at Judith. "Sister Judith, you tell them about the healing God has already given them. They only need to claim it."

Judith held up a white cloth. "When Jesus was placed in the tomb following his crucifixion, the disciples wrapped his body in a linen cloth much like this one. Pastor MacClaren and I were in Jerusalem this past winter. We went to the tomb where Jesus had been laid. I placed this linen cloth near the place that our Lord's precious body had been laid. Pastor MacClaren and I and the army of prayer warriors we had with us prayed over this cloth. We asked God to bless this cloth so that anyone that pinned a piece of it to their clothing would be healed of whatever disease or infirmity they suffered."

"Tell them, Sister, tell them what happened."

Judith's mouth quivered with emotion as she continued. "We took the cloth back to our home in Mexico. There was a young boy there that was terminally ill with a childhood cancer. I cut off a piece of the cloth and attached it to his shirt. One week later he went to the doctor for his appointment and the doctors were all amazed. The boy's cancer was gone."

"OH, PRAISE GOD!" Pastor MacClaren shouted.

"Yes, thank you Jesus. And now, friends, we want to share a piece of this cloth with you. I only need you to send a self-addressed stamped envelope. Enclose a check or money order for twenty-five dollars. We need to pay our workers. They will be carefully cutting this cloth into one-inch strips to send to you. Instructions on how to wear it will be included. Your healing could be as near as a twenty-five dollar check. But you must hurry because the number of strips we can cut from the cloth is limited. Once it's gone it's gone." An address for a post office box scrolled across the screen. A disclaimer was added. *No pieces of the healing cloth will be shipped until your check has cleared our bank.*

"That's all just wonderful. Now don't forget to come to the Falls City Sports Arena this coming Sunday night. God has more riches in store for you than you can imagine. It's His promise. But you have to know how to claim them. Meet us there on Sunday night and we'll teach you how to reach out and receive the blessings that already belong to you. This is Pastor Melvin MacClaren."

"And I'm Sister Judith MacClaren."

"And we'll see you this Sunday night. Come and claim the abundant riches God wants to pour out on you." The screen froze on a photo of the Sports Arena. The announcer gave the details for the Sunday night event. Instructions for ordering the piece of miracle linen repeatedly scrolled on the screen.

"Rose, are you still there?"

"I'm here."

"Well, what do you think about all that?

"You want to know what I really think?"

"Absolutely. Tell me."

"I think that you are the blessing that God had in store for me. And I am so thankful."

"That's nice. I feel the same way about you. I thank God every day for sending you into my life."

Rose giggled.

"Well, that wasn't supposed to be funny. I meant it."

"I know. I was just thinking that if I am the blessing that God had in mind for you, then you're getting shortchanged."

"How's that?"

"I don't have any money."

The Magnolia Series

Dennis R. Maynard

CHAPTER

9

"Father Austin, are you sure you should be over here working today?" Steele's longtime secretary, Crystal, was concerned about her boss. "I'm surprised your wife let you out of the house. You just got out of the hospital yesterday. I think you should be home resting."

Steele smiled, "Thanks for your concern, Crystal, but I assure you I'm just fine. I do have a slight headache, but other than that the doctors told me there is no reason I can't go back to work. Besides, I'd rather be working. At least that keeps my mind off the entire affair."

"So you've heard some of the rumors?"

"What rumors?"

"That you and Mrs. Willoughby were having an affair."

Steele sank back in his chair. "What?"

"Oh, Father Austin, as soon as word got out you were in the hospital, the switchboard lit up. People were calling to ask us to confirm the news."

"What news?"

"Well, it seems the only part of the story that everyone got straight was that you were in the hospital. All agreed that it had something to do with the Willoughby house."

"And beyond that?"

"Are you sure you want to hear this?"

"Crystal, you know I'm going to hear it all eventually. Just give me a few of the highlights."

"Okay, but only because you asked."

"Go on." Steele took a sip of the coffee from the cup on his desk.

"Well, perhaps the most harmless was that you'd had a heart attack or a stroke."

Steele choked on his coffee. He cleared his throat and swallowed. He mused, "If that's the least harmful, I can't wait to hear the worst. Were you able to convince all the callers that wasn't true?"

"Yes, but that may not have helped."

"Why?"

"Because as soon as we'd tamped that one down, they started to believe one of the other rumors."

"Like what?"

"Well again, one of the worst is that you'd had a stroke and died. We were refusing to confirm it until Randi and the children had been told."

"Oh, my God. Please tell me you were able to get that one corrected."

"Father Austin, we did what we could. I've never seen anything like it. All the telephone lines into the church office were blinking. We even had some people come here to the office wanting information."

"Okay. I really appreciate everything you and the staff did to deal with the rumor mill. I will go to each person this morning and personally thank them."

"Father Austin, there is one rumor we weren't able to silence. I think it was being repeated by folks that wanted it to be true."

Steele frowned. "Oh Lord, please have some mercy. What was it?"

Crystal squirmed in her chair. "I suppose it's my duty to let you know. It was the first one I told you about."

"That Mrs. Willoughby and I were having an affair?"

"Only worse."

Steele forced a chuckle. "What could be worse?"

"That Mister Willoughby came home and caught the two of you in bed. He beat you so badly that EMS and the police had to be called. He put you in the hospital."

"And when you tried to squash that one how did people respond?"

"That they expected us to deny it, but they'd heard it on good authority."

"I pushed each caller to give me the name of the person

spreading such malicious gossip, but they refused to tell me. They said they had to protect their anonymous sources, but they believed them."

"Lord Jesus, just when I thought things were settling down in this parish."

"I'm sorry, Father Austin. What else can I do to help?"

"It sounds like you're already doing it. Just continue to counter the rumors with the facts. I did collapse, but the doctors don't know why. They're still waiting on the results of some tests."

"I'll make sure everyone in the office is on the same page. Do you want me to hold all your phone calls? I've already canceled your appointments for today and tomorrow. I know you didn't ask me to do that, but I wanted you to have time to recuperate."

"Thanks, Crystal. You've always done the right thing when it comes to my schedule. I'd like to return my telephone calls. I don't want to get too far behind on those."

"As you might expect, you have quite a stack."

"How many make a stack?"

"I've got twenty-two phone calls for you to return and the day has just begun."

"Okay, let me have them."

Steele thumbed through the pink slips. He let out a low groan. "I guess I might as well start with this one. I'll get the one I least want to return out of the way first. See if you can get him on the line."

Crystal's voice came over the intercom. "Father, Mister Mitchell is on line one."

"Thanks."

Steele picked up his receiver. "This is Father Austin."

"Hmp. And this is The Honorable and Venerable Colonel Mitchell. So you've become so important you can't dial your own telephone. You need to have *The Help* do it for you." Steele could hear the bitterness in his voice.

"What can I do for you, Mister Mitchell?"

"You can add me to the vestry agenda for the meeting

next week."

"It's not that easy. The executive committee of the vestry sets the agenda. It's based on items and reports that have come up through the various vestry committees. They only come before the vestry for confirmation or action."

"Now you get this, Mister Rector, I'm not interested in hearing about the bureaucracy you've set up in my church. If you'd spend as much time studying the scriptures and saying your prayers as you do organizing committees, we'd all be better for it."

"Mister Mitchell, if you want to be on the vestry agenda, you will need to first go to the appropriate vestry committee and present your case to them."

"Well, we'll see about that. I'm putting you on notice that not only will I be at the next vestry meeting, but so will several others. And Mister Rector, we will be heard." With that, Colonel Mitchell slammed down his telephone receiver.

"Father Austin, the bishop is on line four."

Steele shuddered. He knew what he wanted. That malicious rumor about his affair with Virginia Willoughby had made it all the way to the diocesan office in Savannah. "Steele, this is Sean Evans."

"Yes, Bishop. I'm not surprised to get your call."

"I know that what's being reported to me is not true. I know it's not true because I know you. Please tell me what is true."

Steele filled the bishop in on his experience at the Willoughby house. He advised him that the doctors were still waiting on some lab tests before drawing any conclusions. "I really don't know what else to tell you. As of right now you know all that I know."

"I have to ask, did the woman's husband assault you?"

Steele laughed. "No bishop, he's been very supportive and concerned for my health. There was no altercation. Sean, I want to know what happened to me as much as anyone. No, I want to know more than anyone else. I was relieved to learn that I did not have a heart attack or a stroke.

Obviously, I blacked out, that much is true, but beyond that I don't know anything."

"I'm thankful to hear that they ruled those things out, but I'm still concerned for you."

"Thanks. I appreciate that."

"Steele, we've just got to do something to shut down the rumor mill."

"Any suggestions?"

"Yes, use your pulpit. Call them out. Counter them with the facts at your disposal."

"That sounds like good advice. Thanks, Sean. I'll do just that. By the way, how's Eze?"

"He's just great. We're very happy."

"And I'm happy for both of you. Please remember me to him."

"I'll do that. Steele, call me when you know what happened. I'll do all I can from my end to put a stop to the gossip, but I'm not in the ring of fire. You are."

"I know. I've dealt with rumors before, but this time they seem to be taking on a life of their own."

"I'm still confused by people who will accept gossip as gospel."

"That's a great way of putting it. I think I just might use that very expression and take full credit for it."

"It's all yours. Bless you, Steele. Give Randi and your children a hug for me. Call me when you know something."

"Thanks for calling. And thanks for believing in me."

The Magnolia Series

Dennis R. Maynard

10

The canonically elected members of the vestry of First Church are under the impression that they're the final authority in all things pertaining to the parish. They could not be more wrong. They have yet to learn the difference between authority and power. The real power at First Church rests with the First Church Altar Guild.

The members of the altar guild meet monthly. Most every lady on the altar guild is married to one of the men on the vestry. It's at breakfast on the days that the vestry meets that the respective husbands receive their voting instructions from their wives.

While there are well over two hundred members of the First Church Altar Guild, only twelve are invited to the monthly meeting. These twelve are the senior members. They have worked themselves up to this point of personal privilege over the decades. They are following in the steps of their great grandmothers, grandmothers, and mothers. They've earned their stripes. It all began when they were young women going through Junior League training. Now they're the power at First Church. This elite group is the only assembly in the entire congregation that can keep the rector awake at night.

"Have you all heard the latest?" If there was a delicious piece of gossip making the rounds in Falls City, Martha Dexter was privy to it. She also was the most enthusiastic purveyor of all things titillating. Since Almeda Alexander Drummond was absent from this particular meeting, Martha Dexter felt empowered to share this latest bit of juicy news. She knew that Almeda had constantly defended the rector. If she were present she would strongly reprimand Martha for repeating such a malicious rumor. Almeda was not there. Martha decided to seize on the opportunity.

"What?" Several members repeated.

After all, the entire purpose of the monthly meeting was to learn the latest tidbits making the rounds. Of course, the minutes reflected that the meeting was used to plan the details of worship at First Church. Very little time was devoted to those intricacies. It was much more stimulating to hear the latest attacks on the newest victim. It was so much better when the character attacks were directed at a person of some importance. The monthly meetings upstaged the attempts of every twenty-four hour cable show to destroy their favorite political target.

"I have it on very good authority that the rector has been having an affair with a member of this congregation."

"No, you don't say? Several members grasped at their breasts with their hands and inhaled great gusts of air. "Say it isn't so," others pleaded.

Mary Alice Smythe, the long serving chair of the altar guild, challenged Martha. "From whom have you heard this?"

"I'm sorry, Mary Alice, but I promised not to reveal my source."

"I don't believe it," Mary Alice was having nothing to do with attacks on the rector. "I demand that you tell us who told you this malicious untruth."

"I can't tell you who told me, but I have it on very good authority. I completely trust the person that informed me. They saw the two of them together."

"Who? I demand that you tell us!" Mary Alice was losing her temper.

"I can't tell you who told me, but I can tell you who the woman is."

"Alright, who is she?"

"Virginia Willoughby."

"Nonsense." Mary Alice insisted, "That woman is nothing but a promiscuous slut and we all know it. If Father Austin were to ever be unfaithful to his wife, and I don't believe he ever would, it would not be with a tramp like her."

Martha was not about to be hushed. "Well, you can believe what you want to believe, but I have evidence."

Mary Alice raised her eyebrows. "And just what kind of evidence do you possess?"

"My maid's sister works as a cleaning woman at the hospital. My maid's sister told my maid who told my yard man that the rector was taken to the emergency room the other day."

"For what?" Mary Alice asked.

"My maid's sister told my maid who told my yard man that the rector was there being treated for black eyes and a broken arm."

"What are you telling us? I don't believe it." Mary Alice was disgusted by this piece of gossip.

"Okay, you just wait and see. The next time you see Mister Austin, he's going to be sporting two black eyes and a broken arm."

"And just how was he supposed to have received these injuries?"

"Mister Willoughby came home and caught the two of them in the act. He beat the rector so badly that they had to call EMS."

"And how do you know that?"

"My neighbor's youngest daughter is married to one of the EMS attendants."

"And this attendant witnessed these injuries?" Mary Alice queried.

"No, he wasn't on that particular call, but he heard it from one of the attendants that was. He told my neighbor's daughter's husband and she told me."

"I'm sorry. I don't want to believe any of it, but I'm afraid from what you're telling us it just might be true. Ladies, we must be careful not to repeat any of this."

Of course every woman present nodded in agreement. The list of people they each wanted to telephone as soon as the meeting was over flashed before them.

The Magnolia Series

Dennis R. Maynard

CHAPTER

11

Randi Austin was in tears. She'd returned home from grocery shopping at the popular *Side Street Market*. "Honey, what's wrong?" Steele wrapped his arms around her. "Let's sit down. Tell me what happened."

"Oh, Steele, it was just so eerie. The minute I walked into the store I could feel people staring at me."

"Are you sure they were staring at you or was it your imagination?"

Randi wiped her tears with the back of her hand. She raised her voice and clinched her fists. "Steele Austin, I'm not paranoid! I know when people are staring at me with pitiful looks on their faces."

"Randi, I'm not saying you're paranoid. It's just with everything that's been going on, I think we both can be overly sensitive when we're out in public."

"Steele, Mary Alice Smythe and Martha Dexter were at *The Market*."

"There are a couple of gossip mongers for sure. Those two have a pretty solid track record."

"Steele, do you think they're the authors of that awful story about you and the Willoughby woman?"

"No, I really don't believe they're the type to make it up. I do think they enjoy a good piece of scuttlebutt a little more than the average person. I don't think they're the authors of this latest bit of scandal."

"How do you know?"

"I know they're friends. And I really believe that the two of them like us. They may even love us, but they just can't resist any scrumptious piece of hearsay."

"Well, that might shed a little light on the conversation."

"Did they mention it to you?"

"No, but I know they're aware of it."

"How?"

"They never mentioned the rumor. They just tilted their heads to the side with that pity look."

"Oh, I know that look. I hate it."

"Me too. They just said that they were keeping both of us in their prayers."

"Well, that sounds innocent enough."

"That was. It's what they added that upset me."

"Tell me."

"They said that they really hoped that for the sake of our children and First Church, we'd be able to work everything out and keep our marriage together."

Steele squeezed her hand. "Now I understand why you are so upset."

"Steele, are we going to have to move?"

"Oh Randi, we've been through worse than this and we're stronger because of everything we've gone through. All of this is the by-product of living in a glass house."

"Well Steele, I'm tired of it."

"I know. It does get old."

"Steele, I know we've already gone over it. I do accept your explanation. But please tell me again why you went over there. I warned you about that woman. I really need to hear it all one more time."

"I got a telephone call at the office from her. She asked me to come over and have lunch with the two of them. Her husband was going to give me a check for the balance of the Habitat House."

"Then why didn't he just mail it to you?"

"I believe she said he had some questions he wanted to discuss with me."

"What else do you remember? She asked me if I liked *Monte Cristo* sandwiches. She said her housekeeper was going to make them for lunch."

"So her housekeeper was going to be there?"

Steele's eyes lit up. "Randi, I just remembered. Yes, her housekeeper opened the door. She escorted me into their library."

"Did you see Mister Willoughby?"

"No, I don't remember seeing Mister Willoughby."

"What is the last thing you remember?"

"Randi, I told Chief Sparks that ringing their doorbell was the last thing I remembered. When I woke up I was in the hospital." He took Randi's hand and kissed it. "You were there."

"What about the tests that they ran?"

"I only agreed to them because Stone and Chief Sparks insisted. I have to confess I do remember agreeing to them, but I'm not sure I understand why they were necessary."

"When will the results be back?"

"I think they said in a few days."

"But your health is good?"

"Randi, you heard them. The doctors saw nothing that concerned them. Other than passing out, they said I appeared to be completely healthy."

"Steele, what can we do about that awful rumor?"

"Bishop Evans told me I needed to address it from the pulpit this Sunday in my sermon."

"Are you?"

"I've been working on the best way to do it."

"Is that possible? Is there ever an effective way to shut down malicious gossip?"

"I hope so, but I seriously doubt it. Once the damage is done it is irrevocable."

The Magnolia Series

Dennis R. Maynard

12

Mrs. Almeda Alexander Drummond, wife of The Reverend Doctor Horace Drummond and senior associate at First Church, had long ago resolved that she had impeccable taste in all things. For this reason alone, she determined that she should be in charge of the wedding reception for Rose MacClaren and Elmer Idle. While their wedding was not going to be the social event of the season, she was going to make sure Falls City's finest would be in attendance at the reception. The elite of Falls City would be expecting only the finest of all things. This would be especially true when it became known that she was in charge.

Almeda had devoted the past few weeks to flying in chefs from around the country. She was only interviewing the ones with stellar reputations. She wanted to employ a chef for the reception. It was critical that the chef of her choice be one that she could work with. Using one of the caterers that routinely manage these events in Falls City was out of the question. Almeda wanted to put her special mark on this reception. The wedding would be a private affair, but she was determined that the reception would be memorable.

"Let me understand. You say that you have worked in *The White House*." Almeda stared over the top of her glasses at the chef candidate sitting before her. "And you are talking about **the** *White House* in Washington, D.C.?"

"Yes, ma'am."

"You're sure that you prepared meals for the President of the United States?"

"Yes ma'am."

"And you're trying to tell me you were in charge of *State Dinners*?"

"Yes, ma'am, I was."

"And your very best suggestion for a Southern Wedding

Reception is *Tournedos Heloise*?"

"Yes, but we'd begin with a *Salmon Mousse*."

She released a great breath of air from her lungs. "And with all your experience, you are convinced those items would be well-received at a wedding reception in the Confederate South?" Almeda was trying to disguise her true feelings about his recommendations.

"Yes, ma'am. The honored guests at *The White House* always favorably reviewed these entrees."

"Have you ever been to South Georgia?"

"No"

Almeda was amused. "Have you ever read a scholarly work on our glorious Southern history?"

"No ma'am, but I have read history books on the United States."

"Of course you have. Books written by liberal Yankee college professors would be my guess. They have absolutely no appreciation for all that we Southerners have suffered at the hands of the brutal Yankee army."

The chef was confused. "Was there a recent invasion I haven't heard about?"

"Of course not." Almeda was exasperated. "I'm talking about that awful General Sherman that marched through our lovely state burning everything he encountered."

"Were you here?"

Almeda stared at the man in disbelief. "Oh for the sake of everything that's holy. Of course not, I'm talking about the War for Southern Independence. Exactly what school did you attend?"

"I graduated from the finest culinary arts school in my home state of New York."

"I might have known. Did they not teach you anything about the Confederate States of America?"

The chef's eyes brightened. "Oh yes, you people are the ones that tried to keep all the African Americans in chains so they could be your slaves."

Almeda felt her face blush red as the anger rose up in

her chest. "Clearly, you've received a prejudiced and slanted brainwashing. That's a mighty poor excuse for an education. Do you know anything about states rights?"

"About what?"

"That the individual states have the right to determine their own destiny and make their own laws." Almeda shook her head. "Never mind. Clearly I can't undo the lobotomy you received at the hands of your so-called professors. I reject your first suggestions. Can you do any better? Keep in mind we're talking about a *Southern Reception*. You do know what I mean? A *Southern Reception* as contrasted to the way they do things in that pagan land up North."

The chef realized that his suggestions were not being well received. He knew he needed to come up with something more Southern. He remembered another menu he'd used at a state dinner in *The White House*. He brightened. "What about *Arroz con Pollo*?"

Almeda could not hide her irritation. "Have I not made it clear to you that we will be preparing a menu for a Southern wedding?"

"Yes ma'am, you did. One of the Presidents from Texas requested on more than one occasion that we serve *Arroz con Pollo* at our *State Dinners*."

Almeda let out a deep breath and closed her interview notebook. She removed her reading glasses. "Not all the Presidents that have resided in our White House can be credited with having impeccable taste. This is not South Texas. This is South Georgia. We take our traditions and history quite seriously. Okay, this is your last chance. Do you know how to make *Corn Pone?*"

"What is this *Corn Pone?* I've never heard of it."

"No, I don't suppose that anyone educated north of the Mason-Dixon Line would know how to make it."

"North of the what?"

"I'm looking for a chef that knows how to prepare an appropriate reception dinner that complements our Southern Heritage. Obviously, you are not he. Thanks for your time.

My houseboy will walk you to the door." With that, Almeda pushed the button on the floor underneath her table.

"Horace, I don't know what I'm going to do about a chef." Almeda immediately telephoned her husband at the office once the last candidate left.

"Honey, you already have a chef. I think he's excellent. Why are you putting yourself through all this? You know his work. You trust him. He's sufficiently intimidated by you to follow your every instruction to the letter."

"Horace, I've never intimidated anyone."

Doctor Drummond snickered. "Okay, if you say so. I doubt any of us truly see ourselves as others see us."

"I suppose you're right. But I'm also going to need a manager to oversee the physical arrangements."

"Okay, who do you know that has an eye for meticulous detail?"

"Well, the first person that comes to mind is Mary Alice Smythe. But of course, I'd have to follow up on her because she does let some specifics slide."

"Almeda, Honey, I love you."

"And I love you. Now drop the other shoe."

"No matter who you employ you're going to follow up on them. Nothing short of perfection will suit you."

Almeda giggled. "I guess you're right."

"So what's next?"

"I need to make a plan."

"Okay, good luck."

"Wait! How's Steele doing?"

"Our paths crossed in the hallway a few minutes ago. He said he was still feeling a little foolish, but he's fine."

"I'll telephone Randi. I need to check on her."

"Almeda Drummond, you're a good woman. Every day that goes by you give me yet another reason to remember just why I'm so desperately in love with you."

The Magnolia Series

Dennis R. Maynard

CHAPTER

13

"Bernice, where's Mrs. Willoughby?"

"She's gone to the beauty parlor." Bernice was in the kitchen preparing dinner for the Willoughbys. She dreaded the time that she would be left alone with Mister Willoughby. She was afraid that he would ask her questions about the preacher falling sick here at their house. Mrs. Willoughby had already told her what to say if Mister Willoughby ever asked her any questions about it. She'd also paid her a full week's wages to express her appreciation.

"Bernice, I have some questions for you."

She felt a chill run up her spine. "Yes, suh."

"Is your church planning to build a Habitat House with First Church?"

Bernice remembered the answer Miss Virginia had told her to give if anyone asked. "I'sa supposed to get information for de' pastor."

"So if I called your pastor he'd confirm that?"

Bernice hesitated and then shook her head.

"Were you here when Father Austin passed out?"

"No, suh. One of my chillun' got sick. I had to go over to the school to fetch him and take him home."

"Did you prepare lunch for the three of you?"

"Yes suh, I'sa fixed some *Monte Cristo* sandwiches."

Thackston's intuition as a trial attorney kicked in. As long as Bernice had worked for him she'd never prepared a *Monte Cristo* sandwich. "Gosh, that sounds good. I think I'd like to have one now. Please make me one of those *Monte Cristo* sandwiches."

"If'n you's want." Bernice pulled out the meat drawer in their refrigerator and began sorting through the packages of meat. "Mistuh Willoughby, I'sa don't think we got none that *Monte Cristo* meat."

"Oh, what kind of meat do we have?"

"Let me see. We's got pimento loaf, some ham, and a little roast beef."

"No *Monte Cristo* meat?"

"No suh."

"I've forgotten. What color is *Monte Cristo* meat?"

Bernice took in a deep breath. "I'sa guess it be brown."

"What do you put on a *Monte Cristo* sandwich?"

"I'sa use *Duke's Mayonnaise*, lettuce, and tomato."

"And which bread did you use to make the sandwiches the other day?"

"I'sa use white bread just like always."

"And what were you going to serve with it?"

"Baked beans." Bernice blurted out the answer in hopes there would be no more questions.

"And for dessert? What did you prepare for desert?"

Once again, Bernice blurted the first answer that came to her mind, "*Rhubarb Pie*."

That was the last piece of evidence that Thackston needed. He knew that Virginia hated *Rhubarb Pie*. He also knew that Bernice was lying to him. She was simply doing as his wife had instructed.

"Sit down, Bernice."

"Yes, suh." Clearly Bernice was upset. Her eyes were watering and she was wringing her hands.

"Bernice, you're not in trouble with me, but I have to tell you that I know you are not telling me the truth. I know that you don't know how to make a *Monte Cristo* sandwich."

"No, suh, I don't."

"I also know the school did not telephone you to pick up one of your children. I talked to the school."

"Oh, my. Ohhh my. Lord Jesus, help me. I'sa so sorry I lied to you, Mister Willoughby. You's always been so good to Bernice."

"Calm down, Bernice. I told you that you're not in trouble. I'm just trying to figure out what happened to Father Austin when he was here."

"I'sa don't know what happened to that poor man. I wasn't here."

"Where were you?"

Bernice's eyes grew wide and then she looked down at the floor. "Miss Virginia gave me the whole afternoon off. I'sa went to the dog track."

Thackston chuckled. "Wonderful. How did that go? Did you have fun?"

"Yes, suh. I'sa wins twenty dollars."

"Bernice, you never need to mention our conversation to Mrs. Willoughby. It never happened. Do you understand?"

"Yes, suh, but what if she asks?"

"Like I said, we never talked."

"If'n you's say so."

"I do. Now I'll let you get back to your work."

Back in his study, Thackston settled into his desk chair and leaned back. He now knew beyond a shadow of a doubt that his wife had been lying to him. She had done so with such conviction he'd wanted to believe her. He couldn't help but wonder just how many other times she'd lied to him. What else had she lied to him about? Was their entire relationship a lie? Why? He needed to find out. He leaned forward and slapped his desk. He knew what he needed to do. He was going to get to the truth. He picked up his desk telephone.

The Magnolia Series

Dennis R. Maynard

CHAPTER

14

Steele was in the vesting sacristy preparing for the first Solemn High Mass of the day. The verger opened the door. "Everything is ready, Father Austin."

"Did you have the ushers distribute the slips of paper?"

"Yes, Father. They randomly handed out the fifty slips just as you said."

"And they did so with the instructions I gave you?"

The verger chuckled. "Exactly as you instructed. I just can't wait to see what you're going to do with them."

Steele smiled. "Okay, let's go." Steele took his seat in the chair nearest the pulpit. Mother Graystone was presiding at the service. She had just finished censing the altar. Steele breathed in the scent of the holy smoke and thought how very calming and mystical it was. After Deacon Smith read the gospel appointed for the day, Steele climbed the pulpit steps. He smiled at the congregation. "Doesn't it feel good?"

He continued, "Now I know that some of you don't know what I'm talking about. Fifty of you do. You're the ones that received a folded piece of paper when you entered the church this morning. You think you know something that the rest of the congregation doesn't know. You are the lucky ones. You are the very first people to have the information on the sheet. Now doesn't that feel good?" Steele paused and smiled again. "Will all of you that received that little sheet of paper please stand and hold that piece of paper in the air over your heads?"

Fifty people stood and did as he'd instructed. "It feels so good, doesn't it?" Big smiles spread across their faces and they nodded their heads. "Now when you were given that sheet of paper you were also given a verbal instruction by the usher and that instruction was repeated in print on the sheet." Steele nodded and smiled again. "If you recall getting those instructions, you can now be seated." All fifty people sat back down.

Steele chuckled. "Now will anyone that was not given a sheet of paper, but now knows what is printed on it please stand." People all over the nave stood. "Now that you know the news printed on the sheet, aren't you excited? If so, please give yourselves a round of applause." The church echoed with the applause. There were lots of smiles and nods.

"Okay, please be seated. Now let me begin with the fifty people that received a sheet. You were told verbally and in writing not to repeat to anyone the news that was printed on the sheet. But obviously, it just felt so good to hear that news you couldn't resist sharing it." There was some uncomfortable laughter in the congregation.

"Okay, that's all understandable. Will all of you that now believe my wife is pregnant with twins please stand?" Several people stood. "Will those of you that think she is pregnant with triplets stand?" More people stood. "Will those of you that believe Randi is pregnant with quintuplets please stand?" Still more people stood. "Don't those of you in the congregation not included in this juicy bit of news feel left out? You were not included in this press release.

Now it's time for the truth. My wife is not pregnant with twins. She's not pregnant with triplets. But..." Steele took a long pause relishing the anticipation before continuing. "She's not pregnant with quintuplets. The truth of the matter is she's not even pregnant. Please, everyone sit down."

Steele realized his voice was becoming stronger and louder. "For the past few days there has been a horrible rumor circulating through this congregation and community. That rumor is an attack on my character and that of a couple in this congregation. I want you to take a good look at me. I don't have any black eyes, my lip is not cut, and my arms are not broken. The best way to combat false gossip is with facts."

Steele glanced out over the congregation. "Now please listen to the facts. A few days ago I made a pastoral visit to the home of a couple in this congregation. Yes, a couple. The husband, wife, and their housekeeper were all present. While there I passed out or fainted. EMS was called. The doctors tell me that it could have been a sudden drop in my blood pressure. Perhaps I suffered a spike in my blood sugar, or a few other possibilities. They ran several tests on me and as of this morning, I'm in perfect health.

Let's return to the news printed on those sheets of paper. It's perfectly understandable that when we hear a juicy bit of news we'll want to be among the first to share it. I don't fault anyone for that. But haven't we all grown tired of twenty-four hour news cycles that are based on anonymous sources? *I have it on good authority from a nameless person.* Aren't we all just sick of it?

Surely the time has come for us to stop accepting as fact news reports that are nothing more than gossip. Can't we see that the purpose of such reporting is not to present facts, but a biased attempt to shape our opinion about another person or issue? It's nothing more than an endeavor to destroy the life and reputation of another person masking as news. Often we can see the bitterness and anger literally seething on the face and in the voice of the person trying to convince us to agree with them.

As Christian people, can we not be the first to stop finding a person guilty by accusation? As Christians we must reject any and all reports that have the sole purpose of destroying another person's good name."

Steele paused. "I know that not many of you think of me as a Shakespearean scholar, but I've managed to struggle through quite a few of his plays." Some in the congregation managed a chuckle. "I'm particularly fond of *Othello*. There is a quote in that play I believe most apropos to this subject. It's attributed to the character *Lago*. He reminds us that honor is one of our most important possessions. Those who attack our honor, our character, and our name are destroying that which has value only to us. Our character and reputation, our name, is useless to anyone else. Listen carefully to what he has to say.

'Good name in man and woman, dear my lord, is the immediate jewel of their souls. Who steals my purse steals trash; 'tis something, nothing; 'Twas mine, 'tis his, and has been slave to thousands; but he that filches from me my good name robs me of that which not enriches him, and makes me poor indeed.'

Think of the damage that anonymous sources and good authorities have done to innocent people's lives, marriages, families, careers, and health. The bloody wounds inflicted on their honor and character will be permanent and irreversible. There will be the inevitable retractions once the information is proven false. But those disclaimers seldom make the lead story on the nightly news. Printed nullifications can only be found in small print on the last pages of the newspaper below the used car ads.

I don't think that the ugly rumor about me and another member of this congregation will dissipate quickly based on my remarks today. I should imagine it will continue to circulate for some time. In some ways the damage has already been done. As with all gossip, there is no way to undo that damage. But I can encourage all of us to start ignoring unsubstantiated rumors and news reports based on anonymous sources. They are nothing more than gossip and we should not repeat them as fact. I ask you to remember that just as I was the target of a malicious rumor every one of you could be subjected to the same kind of assault.

The Book of Proverbs teaches us that our tongues have the power to build up and to tear down. As Christian people, it's time to reject the prevalent atmosphere of anonymous and unnamed sources. May God give us the strength and courage to do so."

The Magnolia Series

Dennis R. Maynard

CHAPTER

15

Henry Mudd concluded the opening meditation at the monthly meeting of the First Church Vestry. He asked the vestry to join him in saying the *Lord's Prayer*. Steele thanked Henry for his devotional and referred the members of the vestry to the evening's agenda that had been previously mailed to them. Just then the conference room doors swung open. In stormed Colonel Mitchell, Howard Dexter, and ten other members of First Church. They took their stations along the walls surrounding the conference table. Stone Clemons spoke first. "Colonel, what is the meaning of this?"

"As I told your rector last week on the phone, we want to speak to the vestry."

"And what did the rector tell you?"

"He gave me a lot of double talk about going to some committee to air our grievances. I believe all vestry meetings are open to the members of the congregation to attend."

"Yes, that is true. We also have a procedure for placing items on our agenda."

"We demand to be heard."

"Colonel, you are disrupting this meeting."

Chief Sparks leaned over and whispered to Stone, "Just say the word and I can get an officer to come over here and escort them out."

Stone shook his head. "I think the better move would be just to hear them out." He glanced at Steele. "With the rector's permission, Colonel, we will agree to give you ten minutes. But at the end of that ten minutes, you are to either be silent for the rest of this meeting or leave."

Steele nodded.

"The rector has agreed. Will you keep your remarks to ten minutes?"

"That won't be a problem. We have our list of demands

right here. I'll read each of them."

"Go on." Clearly Stone was perturbed.

"We demand that the rector of this church immediately begin preaching sermons condemning homosexual marriage and homosexuality. It's a sin. We also demand that this vestry pass a resolution condemning homosexuality and post that resolution in the worship leaflet and the parish newsletter. We further insist that the rector state in his sermons and the vestry state in their resolution that no homosexual marriage shall ever be permitted at First Church. We want every member of the vestry and the rector to sign that resolution individually in a handwriting that is legible."

Several members of the vestry snickered. "Continue", Stone grinned.

"We further demand that a pulpit committee be formed. I will be the permanent chair of that committee and I will choose the members. Every sermon that the rector plans to preach must be submitted to our committee for approval and edit before said sermon is preached. Any edits we make to a proposed sermon are final and the sermon must be preached as our committee has approved it. If he fails to deliver the sermon as we have approved it then his employment at First Church shall end immediately."

Steele started to respond. Stone Clemons tapped his foot underneath the table with his own foot and shook his head. "What else?"

"We demand that this parish restore the all-male priesthood to our ministry. Women may read the scripture lessons, serve the chalice, and be ordained deacons, but no priestess is to be allowed to lead a service in First Church. We do not want women serving as ushers either. That is a ministry that should only be exercised by men."

Steele was having a difficult time controlling his anger. Stone gently patted him on the leg. Steele maintained his silence. Stone shook his head, "Is that all?"

"We have two more demands."

"Continue."

"We demand that no alcohol shall be served at any parish function save the Service of Communion."

Several vestry members couldn't restrain their laughter. "Colonel Mitchell, you actually expect us to take your demand for parish temperance seriously?" Stone was restraining his own laughter.

Colonel smirked, "I don't need to come over here and drink box wine. I think this campus should be alcohol-free."

An amused grin spread across Stone's face, "Are you finished?"

"No, we have a final ultimatum. The rector and vestry shall immediately impose a moratorium on receiving any new members into First Church for three years. I think we can all agree that this parish has simply gotten too big. I don't know where the rector is finding all these new people. They are occupying the very pews that all our families have sat in for generations."

Colonel Mitchell's voice broke with emotion. "Think about it. My great-grandparents bought the pew that my family used to be able to sit in on Sunday mornings. Every one here knew that it was the *Mitchell Pew*. You all respected that and us. I didn't sit in your family pew and you didn't sit in mine. But now look at what this man has done to our church. People that are not even dressed properly for a First Church worship service are desecrating all our family pews. All of our ancestors would be so ashamed. Don't you agree with me that these people don't belong in our parish? They are not our kind. First Church used to be a church for the finest citizens of Falls City and the Great State of Georgia. You only have to look around on Sunday to see that our membership standards under this rector have been disturbingly lowered."

"Now are you finished?"

"We are."

"I'm not." Henry Mudd was agitated. "As a member of this vestry, I will not agree to any of your demands. They are bigoted and mean-spirited."

Colonel grinned, "Of course someone like you with your

family history would suggest our demands are bigoted."

"And just what do you mean by that?"

"I shouldn't have to explain it to you."

"And I suggest that you, sir, choose your next words very carefully." Henry had risen from his chair and was pointing his finger at Colonel Mitchell.

Colonel shouted, "I want to know if this vestry is going to do as we have asked."

Stone had lost his patience. "Sir, you did not ask us to study these issues and report back to you. You have made demands. I, for one, don't respond well to demands."

"We want to hear from the rector. Do you or do you not agree with our position on these important issues?" Colonel Mitchell already knew the answer to his question. He just wanted to get Steele on record.

Steele glanced over at Stone. Stone nodded for him to respond. "I think the critical word that you have used is issues. A couple of them are really quite complex. You are asking the vestry and me to give you simplistic answers to complex questions. The larger Episcopal Church has already addressed some of the issues you have presented. I see no reason for us to revisit them."

"More double talk." Colonel Mitchell smirked.

"No, Mister Mitchell, it's not double talk. As Christians, we must base our decisions on the values Jesus taught and not get bogged down in political issues."

"And you would have us believe that you know the difference?" Colonel Mitchell clearly was mocking Steele.

"Okay, let's look at it this way. A Christian value is that which undergirds the position that the Church might take on an issue. For example, the Church has come to understand that God is more concerned about what is in a person's heart than He is the makeup of their genetic chromosomes. That led us, as Episcopalians, to ordain women as priests and bishops."

"Well, I don't agree."

"And no one is going to force you to do so."

"What about all the gays?"

"Again, the value that guides that decision is the way Jesus welcomed all who came to him. He turned no person away. He welcomed everyone. He never asked them to state their political party, their financial status, their race, or their sexuality before receiving them into his loving embrace."

"Well, you're wrong on that one too."

"Mister Mitchell, the values that Jesus taught us should be the foundation for all of our decisions. As a priest, I choose not to preach on the many controversial issues that are loaded with emotion. I prefer to teach the values that Christ taught us. If I do a sufficient job doing that, then our faithful will be able to make decisions based on those values. They'll not get caught up in whatever mob mentality is currently looking for simplistic answers to complex questions."

"So what you all are saying is that you're not going to do as we've asked."

Stone glanced over at the Steele and nodded for him to answer. "Clearly, I've not done a sufficient job teaching the values that would undergird any of these decisions. I can promise you I will try to do better. As you've demonstrated here tonight, issues divide us, but if we focus on the values that Jesus taught us, the issues take care of themselves."

Colonel shook his head. "But you're not going to do any of the things we've listed."

"I'm afraid not."

"Then we're through here. But before we leave, you all need to know that this isn't over."

The Magnolia Series

Dennis R. Maynard

16

The Falls City Sports Arena was packed to capacity. A twelve-piece orchestra accompanied a choir of well over one hundred voices. The participants were volunteers from several Evangelical congregations in the surrounding communities. They opened the service. The words to the various *Praise Hymns* were projected onto the giant screens on all four sides of the arena. Melvin and Judith had carefully planned and choreographed the service. The choir was to begin the service with meditative hymns. These were designed to calm the packed arena and help the worshippers to focus. Some of those gathered held their hands in the air and swayed gently in their seats.

As the time for The Reverend Melvin MacClaren's and his wife, Judith's, appearance grew near, the music became more praise-worthy and uplifting. The worshippers rose to their feet and clapped their hands rhythmically to the music. The praise hymn immediately before Melvin and Judith walked onto the flower-strewn stage had every person in attendance worked up to a feverish pitch.

Just when it appeared that the atmosphere in the arena could not become any more electric, the jumbotrons projected a larger than life photo of Melvin and Judith. Underneath their photo were the words *God Is Going To Bless You Tonight!* After seeing those words the huge arena reverberated with applause and shouting. Magically, a smiling Melvin and Judith walked through a screen of gray smoke and appeared on the stage. Spotlights washed over them and all the people in the arena. There was an explosion of indoor fireworks across the stage. The orchestra conductor directed the instrumentalists to a full *forte*. It was deafening.

As the music began to subside, the fireworks ceased, and the applause began to die down. Melvin shouted into the headset microphone he was wearing, "GAWD IS GOING TO BLESS YOU TONIGHT!" That was followed by more applause and shouts.

As that jubilation began to wane he shouted, "PLEASE GREET MY BEAUTIFUL WIFE, JUDITH!" Once again, the applause rose as Judith smiled and waved at the crowd. "Thank you, Pastor MacClaren." She gently cooed in a voice dripping with honey, "God is going to give every person here a special blessing this very night." The audience responded with more applause.

Melvin turned to the look at the musicians. "Choir, this congregation wants to claim the blessings God has for them." More words appeared on the screen as the melody for a jubilant hymn began. Hands went up all over the arena. Melvin and Judith threw their hands into the air. They began to sway together as all in the place sang at the top of their voices, *"The blessing is mine. I claim the blessing that is mine. Thank you, Lord Jesus, the blessing is mine."*

After the words to the hymn had been repeated several times, Pastor MacClaren asked that all present be seated. "Tonight, Judith and I are going to teach you how to claim the blessings that God already has in store for you. As Jesus promised, he wants to give you life and to give it to you more abundantly. He wants you to live. He does not want you to live day to day. He does not want you to live paycheck to paycheck. He does not want your marriage to be lifeless. If you are alone, God has already chosen that perfect man or woman for you. If you are crippled or ill, God wants you to be made whole. Our Lord God wants to give you all this and so much more. Do you trust and believe in our majestic God?"

Once again the congregation exploded with applause and shouts of *"Amen"* and *"Praise the Lord"*.

Judith continued the teaching, "But you have to know how to claim these blessings. They are already waiting on you. But if you don't claim them you will never receive them. Pastor MacClaren and I want to teach you how to claim them. The first step in claiming these blessings is to acknowledge just how wondrous and powerful our glorious God is. Do you believe He is wondrous?" The congregation once again rose to their feet with applause. As that died down, she shouted, "DO YOU BELIEVE HE IS ALL POWERFUL?" There was more applause. "DO YOU BELIEVE HE WANTS TO BLESS YOU?" The shouts and applause were louder than before. Judith pointed at the choir and once again the audience sang with fervor, "*The blessing is mine. I claim the blessing that is mine. Thank you, Lord Jesus, the blessing is mine.*"

"Thank you, Jesus. You have just learned the first step in the process to claim your blessing. You have to believe that our God is powerful enough to give you such a blessing. And now, do you want to know step two?"

The congregation shouted, "YES!"

Judith was pleased with the response. "I want you to close your eyes. Every eye is to be closed. Every head is to be bowed. Now in prayer, I want you to visualize the blessing that God has in store for you. Visualize that job you want. Visualize having a larger paycheck. Visualize having a new house, or a new car, or that vacation you've always wanted. Visualize a happy marriage. Visualize that loving husband or devoted wife that God has already chosen for you. If you are ill, visualize now that our mighty God has healed your body and made you whole. We need to visualize the blessing that God has prepared for you. While the choir sings, I want each head to remain bowed and every eye to remain closed. Choir, help us visualize the blessings God wants to give each of us."

With that the choir began to quietly sing, "*The blessing is mine. I claim the blessing that is mine. Thank you, Lord Jesus, the blessing is mine.*"

After several minutes of meditative singing had passed, Pastor MacClaren whispered into his microphone, "Now open your eyes. Did you see it? Did you see the blessing God wants to give you?"

Immediately every person present rose and shouted, "YES". The applause was deafening.

"Now we only have to claim the blessing God is holding

in His hands for you at this very moment." Pastor MacClaren offered a reassuring smile.

Judith stepped forward and held up a book. "Claiming the blessing requires that we make some changes in our own lives. This is far too much to cover in just one teaching in one night. Pastor MacClaren and I have written this book so that you can refer to the needed action steps over and over again until the blessing is yours. The ushers are now coming down the aisles with copies of this book. For a mere forty dollars the book is yours. That is a small price to pay for the blessing that soon shall be yours. If the ushers should happen to run out of copies of the book, there are booths beside each exit where you can pick up your copy. This book is not available in bookstores, and we do have a limited number of copies with us. You don't want to miss out on getting your copy tonight." Then she asked in her most pastoral voice, "Do you think forty dollars is too much to pay for that new house or car?"

"NO!" The people shouted.

"Is forty dollars too much to pay for a loving spouse, a healing of your body, or a new job?"

"NO!" The crowd shouted even louder than before.

Judith smiled sweetly, "Don't forget that at the booths in the lobby there are pieces of the healing cloth which can also be yours this very night."

Melvin closed the service, "And we thank you for being here. We give thanks to our Almighty God who has a special blessing in store for each of you." With that the choir began to jubilantly sing again, "*The blessing is mine. I claim the blessing that is mine. Thank you, Lord Jesus, the blessing is mine.*" The smoke machines on either side of the stage filled the stage with gray smoke. And just as magically as Melvin and Judith had appeared they were gone. The stage went dark and the arena lights went up. People rushed the ushers and booths for copies of the book.

The Magnolia Series

Dennis R. Maynard

17

Steele slid into the booth opposite one of his best friends in Falls City. The Reverend Josiah Williams was the senior pastor of the largest African American Church in the area. They had agreed to meet at *The Plantation House.* It was a popular restaurant that specialized in all things fried.

Josiah chuckled, "Will your mistress be joining us?"

"Good one. I see you've heard the latest rumor."

Josiah continued to chuckle, "I believe the entire state of Georgia has heard it."

"Well, I'm so happy that my discomfort can give you a little amusement."

"I was surprised to see you walk in here under your own power."

"As you can see, I'm perfectly fine."

"Oh, the way I heard it that husband gave you one royal ass whoopin'."

"Again, I'm so pleased to be able to bring a ray of sunshine into your humdrum existence."

"Okay, I'll not pull your chain any more. Are you okay?"

"I'm fine."

"What are the doctors telling you?"

"They ran a bunch of tests at the hospital, but I haven't heard any results."

"What do you think happened?"

"Honestly Josiah, I don't know. Obviously, something went wrong, but I don't have a clue. Chief Sparks suspects something nefarious happened. I went along with those tests as well. It's a waiting game right now. But I feel just fine. I don't have any memory of the event other than it occurred."

"Well, Rubidoux and I will keep you in our prayers."

"Thanks friend, I really appreciate it." Steele looked around the restaurant. "Did you choose this table?"

"No, this is where they seated me."

"Josiah, this restaurant is more than half empty. They put us right here opposite the bathroom doors."

"I feel fortunate they gave me a table this good. I had the feeling the host would just as soon I eat in the kitchen."

"Well, this is ridiculous. I don't want to eat my meal with aromas from the toilets washing over it."

"Steele, let's not make a scene. I've learned it's just not worth it."

"Believe me there will be no scene, but we're going to move to one of those empty tables."

Steele approached the host. "Excuse me, we'd like to move to another table."

The host examined him from top to bottom. His eyes focused on Steele's clerical collar. "I don't want any trouble, Father."

"Neither do I. We just want another table."

"I didn't know you'd be joining your... uhh, your..."

Steele stopped him. "He's my friend and the pastor of one of the largest congregations in this state."

"If you say so. Well, we can seat you over there." The host pointed to a booth in the far corner.

"No, we'd like to be seated at one of the tables by your front window."

"I'm sorry, but none of those are available."

"All of them are empty."

"We reserve those for our regulars."

Steele lowered his voice. "You said you don't want a scene. My friend and I both pastor churches here in Falls City with a combined membership of nine thousand people. What kind of scene do you think we could make?"

The waiter's face blushed with anger. He glanced down at his reservation sheet. "I believe we might be able to accommodate you after all. Please follow me."

Josiah had been watching the entire scene when he saw Steele motion for him to follow. "Brother, how did you do this?"

"I explained it to him."

"I guess I've just grown used to it. Truthfully, I've grown too tired to constantly challenge every hint of bigotry."

"Josiah, I thought that this country had moved beyond all this."

"I think we have in so many ways, but a few pockets of racism still exist."

"My friend, I don't see your skin color when I look at you. I just see my friend, Josiah."

"Exactly. You've gotten to know me for the person I am. When that happens skin color becomes irrelevant. It's a non-player. But if you didn't know me and you ran into me in a dark parking lot, you'd most likely have a different reaction."

"Understood. But is that racism or a visceral response that is a part of my survival instinct?"

"Say more."

"Okay, have you seen you? You played college football. You're at least six feet five inches tall and you're probably two hundred and fifty pounds of solid muscle. You could squeeze me in a minute."

Josiah chuckled, "And don't you forget it."

"Don't worry about that. I'm not about to challenge you to any kind of wrestling match. But Josiah, is it your color or your size that would cause me to have a visceral response? I mean, would I have the same reaction to someone that is five foot two and weighs ninety-nine pounds?"

"Even if he's black?"

"Okay, let me finish my thought. What if I ran into a six foot five inch white guy weighing two hundred and fifty pounds with neck and arm tattoos and an ugly scruffy beard in that same dark parking lot? I think I would have a similar reaction."

"Point taken. But what label would you place on a host putting a black man at a dining table by the toilets when your restaurant is half empty?"

"Clearly that's exactly why I needed to challenge it. It's pure racism."

"I have a few thoughts on that white guy with the neck

tattoo that you described."

"Okay, shoot."

"True, he could bring a visceral response. But he also could be a loving husband and great father to a couple of kids. You'd just have to get to know him."

"I guess I keep hoping that we can make Doctor King's words a reality. We should judge people by the quality of their character and not the color of their skin."

Josiah chuckled, "Or their neck tattoos. On another subject, did you hear about the big revival Sunday night at the Sports Arena?"

"I fear I'm very familiar with the stars of the show. You'll remember that MacClaren was the pastor at Saint Andrew's Presbyterian."

"I thought he sounded familiar."

"His wife used to be a member of my congregation."

Josiah snapped his fingers. "Okay, I remember. It's all coming back to me. You do realize that the Sports Arena was completely packed?"

"So I heard."

"I know the two of them had an angle, I just don't know what it is."

"They walked out of here with almost a million dollars."

"In one night? How?"

"One of my members was hired to manage all their book concessions. She said they sold almost twenty-five thousand copies of their book Sunday night. She told me that people were falling all over themselves to buy multiple copies. They sold them for forty dollars a copy. That doesn't even include the tee shirts, bumper stickers, magnets, potholders, towels, prayer cloths, and dog bowls they sold. You do the math."

"Wow!"

"Have you cautioned your people about the *Prosperity Gospel*?"

"No, I haven't up to now. That may need to change. I just find it so difficult to believe that any educated person could buy into any of it."

"Well, not all of them are educated."

"I understand. When you were a kid did the traveling medicine show ever come to your town?"

"You mean the one that Cher sings about?"

"Yes, that's the one. Remember their primary product was an elixir that would solve any problem you had. It could grow hair, cure diseases, and make you more potent."

Josiah nodded. "I remember."

"It seems to me that the *Prosperity Gospel* preachers are selling an elixir. They're suggesting that God is like a giant Tylenol. You need only take a large dose of God once a day and all your problems will go away."

"Don't forget that you'll also become rich and the man or woman of your dreams will walk into your life."

A waiter approached their table. "My manager wants to know if you all plan to order food or do you intend to occupy this table all afternoon?"

Josiah glanced up at him and then at Steele. "Father Austin, I think I'm hungry for a deep dish pizza."

The waiter huffed. "We don't serve pizza."

Josiah smiled, "Exactly. Steele, I think we need to eat at a more friendly establishment."

Steele nodded, "Pizza, you say? Let's go."

As the two walked out of the restaurant Josiah put his arm around Steele, "Do you have any idea what they were going to do to our food if we'd eaten there?"

The Magnolia Series

Dennis R. Maynard

18

Rose MacClaren was naked. She was in Elmer Idle's bed lying underneath his silk sheets. Elmer returned to the bedroom carrying a cup of tea and a snack for each of them. "Maybe this will give us enough energy for round two."

Rose giggled. "That's mighty big talk."

"Well, let's just see what happens." Rose and Elmer learned early in their relationship that they had to balance needed time for lovemaking and time for Rose's three children. They extended their lunch hours each day to accomplish the first. They were then able to devote their full attention to the children after school. Elmer had been particularly helpful to Rose's youngest, John Calvin. He had a diagnosed learning disability. It was that very disability that had made him the recipient of his father's abuse. Elmer is the first man that the abused young boy has trusted.

"Have you heard any more about the rally our exes held at the Sport's Arena?"

"One of the girls that works part time for me in the shop attended. She came back all starry-eyed this morning. She described it as 'the greatest thing she's ever done in her life'. She can't believe that I was once married to that 'wonderful man'. Those are her words, not mine."

"Gosh, that must have been tough to hear."

"The toughest part was having to look at the tee shirt she was wearing. It had a large photo of both our exes on the front of it."

"How did you handle that?"

"I just smiled. Why rain on her parade? She wanted to show me a copy of their book. She bought three of them for her family members. Elmer, those books cost her one hundred and twenty dollars. She can't afford that. But she's convinced that if she'll follow all the steps outlined in the book, God will help her find a wealthy husband."

"What's the name of the book?"

"I didn't even notice. I couldn't get past the full-page photo of the two of them on the cover. I'm not even sure it has a name. It doesn't matter. I don't plan on giving them forty dollars for one."

"Has he telephoned you? Do you think he wants to see the children?"

"No. He's not called. I'm not even sure the children will agree to see him. What about her? Has she called you?"

"No. That suits me just fine. I really don't want to hear from her."

"Can we change the subject?"

Rose had finished her cup of tea and was putting it on the bedside table. As she did, the sheet covering her slipped down and exposed her bare shoulder and the top of her breast. Elmer leaned over and kissed her shoulder. "And just what did you have in mind?"

Rose smiled. She re-covered her chest and shoulder with the sheet. "We'll see about that in a minute. Right now I want to talk about our wedding."

Elmer leaned back against his pillows. "Okay. You haven't changed your mind about marrying me, have you?"

"No, Silly. I want to marry you more than ever. I want to talk about Almeda."

"She can be a force to deal with."

"Elmer, she won't let me do anything."

"It's our wedding. Do you want me to talk to her?"

"No. I need to handle this myself."

"I know she wants to pay for everything, and I am grateful. I'd like to have some say in planning the reception. I do have a couple of ideas."

"What does she say when you give her your ideas?"

"She just smiles and pats my hand. She tells me not to worry about details. She'll take care of them. She just wants me to relax and enjoy my wedding day."

"What is your biggest concern?"

"My immediate concern is the shopping trip she has planned. She wants to take us all to Atlanta. She insists on paying for my wedding dress and wedding clothes for each of the children."

"Wow. That's really generous."

"I know. My concern is that she won't let me or the children choose what we want. I know our kids. If they don't like it, they won't agree to wear it."

A smile crossed Elmer's face, "You said 'our kids'."

"Did I? Elmer, Honey, they've asked me if they can call you *Dad*."

A tear ran down Elmer's cheek. "You know that I would love that. In fact, I was going to ask you if I could adopt them as my own."

"I had a hunch that was your plan."

"Don't you have full custody?"

"In the American divorce I do. Remember, he divorced me in Mexico and that decree granted him custody. Mister Clemons had one of his attorneys file for me here in Georgia. I received custody."

"Hmm, I'm just curious. Is he supposed to be sending you child support?"

Rose's eyes widened. "Yes."

"How much?"

"I don't remember exactly. I never figured I'd be able to collect a dime of it anyway. I think its a thousand dollars or so for each child."

"And he knows that?"

"My attorney sent him a copy of the divorce decree to their address in Mexico. We know he got it because he had to sign for it. He has all of that on file in his office."

"You realize that in the State of Georgia if a spouse fails to pay child support they can go to jail?"

"They're probably on their way back to Mexico by now."

"But if they haven't left, the judge can take his passport away from him. He won't be able to go back until he's paid up."

A pleased look washed across Rose's face, "What are you suggesting?"

"I'm just thinking that any man that now lives in a palatial mansion ought to share some of his ill-gained wealth with his children."

Rose put her arms around Elmer's neck. "Mister Idle, I've never loved you more." Elmer gently pulled the sheet off her shoulders. He began to lovingly smother them with gentle kisses.

The Magnolia Series

Dennis R. Maynard

19

"My Christian friends, I want to thank each of you for your attendance this evening." Colonel Mitchell was looking out at a crowd of over two hundred members of First Church. He had mailed a letter to every household on the membership roster. He asked the members if they were concerned about the direction of The Episcopal Church and First Church in particular. He listed four problematic areas.

1. The ordination of women as priests and bishops.
2. The ordination of gay and lesbian clergy.
3. The blessing of gay and lesbian marriages.
4. The sanctity of life and the liberal teachings of the church on abortion and euthanasia.

He was overwhelmed by the response. The conference room he'd booked at the local Marriott was packed to standing room only. "I know from the conversations I've already had with a few of you that not all of you are in agreement with each of these four areas. Personally, if I find even one of them conflicting with God's Holy Word as preserved for us in the Bible, that's too many. The primary reason I called this meeting is that I, for one, have found the liberalization of The Episcopal Church and First Church to be intolerable."

He was pleased to have his remarks interrupted by applause. "I believe it's important to provide you with full disclosure. I, along with a few of the other folks in attendance tonight, took our concerns to the rector and vestry. We politely asked them to address each of the areas I listed for you in my letter. I regret to inform you that both the rector and the vestry were dismissive of our concerns. Basically, they refused to pass a resolution affirming the scriptural and traditional teachings of the church on each of these issues."

A woman on the front row interrupted him. "I do have a problem with three of the issues you've named, but I have no problem with women priests and bishops."

"Well, I do." Another woman responded. "They are doing nothing to help promote the feminine ideal. I don't think women should pretend to be men. Everyone knows that being a priest is a man's job. Clerical collars were designed to be a part of a man's wardrobe. Women have no business wearing one. I believe there is another name for women pretending to be men. Priest or bishop should not be one of them."

Another woman agreed. "I refuse to attend any service being led by that so-called woman priest at First Church."

A man added, "I attend Mass, but I refuse to pass *The Peace* with her and I do not receive the *Holy Bread* from her."

"I've heard some interesting rumors about our current bishop." A man shouted from the back of the room. "Do you know if they're true?"

Colonel Mitchell was pleased. He nodded knowingly, "I've heard the same. Personally, I believe that where's there's smoke there must be fire."

"So what is your plan? What are we supposed to do? Do you want us to sign a petition and send it to the rector?"

A general murmur of agreement rose up in the room. Colonel Mitchell motioned for silence. "I don't think a petition will accomplish a thing. Even if the rector and vestry did acquiesce, the National Episcopal Church in New York has already set a course. I don't see any indication that they plan to deviate from it."

"So what are we to do?" Several people asked at the same time.

"How many of you still support First Church financially?" Most everyone in the room held up their hands.

"Now let me ask how many of you have decreased your financial support?"

Once again, many in the room held up their hands. A woman objected. "I don't contribute to support Father Austin. I give to my church. I don't think we should use our tithes and offerings as a weapon."

Another woman objected, "I don't understand how any

of us could support that man? The money you put in the offering plate goes to pay his ridiculous salary. The rector is systematically destroying our beloved church."

"I write on my pledge card that none of my offering is to go to the diocese or the National Episcopal Church." Colonel Mitchell added.

"Maybe we should all do that." A woman suggested.

Colonel Mitchell nodded. "That brings me to something I'd like to suggest. I want to go back to the rector with a petition signed by the people in this room. Our petition will demand that the vestry stop giving our tithes and offerings to the diocese and National Church."

The room exploded with applause. When it died down Colonel Mitchell added. "I'd also like to give him one more chance to agree to the previous resolutions that we tried to get the vestry to agree to."

"And if they don't?" A woman asked.

"Then we'll meet again. I do have another option, but I'd really like to give the rector and vestry one more chance to do the right thing."

The Magnolia Series

Dennis R. Maynard

20

The Reverend Canon Jim Vernon was furious. His blood had been boiling the last few days. He'd not been able to sleep. He was even having trouble functioning when he had the opportunity to do so at the bathhouse or the club. He lay awake rehearsing over and over in his mind just what he could have done differently. From the moment the two of them walked into the restaurant that night, he knew he had to do something to get even with them. He managed to become their waiter. He gave their food the special treatment reserved for all his rude customers. But they figured it out. They were onto him. What did he say or do to give himself away? What could he have done differently?

They never touched their salads. They never even picked up their forks. Sean and his rabbi simply got up and left the restaurant after paying their check minus a gratuity. He was so furious. The ultimate insult was he had to pay their tip from his own money to the server that was supposed to wait on them.

Nothing seemed to help Jim with his anger. He simply could not believe that Sean had tossed him aside for that rabbi. He had to admit that the rabbi was a bit of a hunk, but Jim considered himself to be pretty desirable. He would never call himself pretty. He was sure that Sean considered his rabbi to be so. Jim thought of himself as rugged. His abs were cut and his biceps had a nice form. The more he compared himself to Sean's new love, the angrier he got. He had to do something.

Perhaps it was the joint that he'd been smoking. Maybe it was the bottle of Irish whiskey he'd just downed. He remembered that is was Sean's favorite. Oh, the very thought of it all was just too much. It could have been the combination of the two. But he picked up the directory of the clergy in the Diocese of Savannah. He ran his finger over the list. Then he knew exactly where to begin. He would call the rector of the most conservative and homophobic parish in the diocese. He picked up his landline and punched in a number. "This is Father Anderson", the voice on the other end answered.

"Do you know that your bishop is a queer?"

"What? Who is this?"

Jim tried not to slur his words. "Do you understand that you're working for a queer?"

"I have no idea who this is, but I don't appreciate your tone."

"I'm trying to do you a favor."

"As I said, I don't know who you are, but I doubt you're trying to do anything for me."

"How does it feel to have a homosexual for a bishop?"

"I'm going to hang up now. I see no further reason to listen to you."

"Wait! This is Jim Vernon."

"Canon Vernon?"

"The one and the same."

"I thought you were fired."

"I was."

"So you actually think that you can get even with your former employer by calling me and defaming him? That's just a bit juvenile."

"I'm trying to expose a liar and a hypocrite."

"Young man, I don't know anything about the bishop's sexuality and quite frankly as long as he doesn't do anything to publicly embarrass this diocese, I could not care less."

"But..."

"Excuse me, Jim, there is no 'but'. The only thing I know about Bishop Evans is that when my wife was in the hospital fighting for her life he came to see her every day. He prayed with her and he comforted my children and me. For that he will have my eternal gratitude."

"Do you understand what I'm trying to tell you? Bishop

Evans likes to ..."

"Jim, stop. I don't want to hear anything else you have to say. Obviously you are hurt because the bishop ended your employment, but that gives you no cause to malign him. I suggest you pick yourself up and find another position."

"I can't. He's blackballed me. None of the bishops in the neighboring dioceses will talk to me."

"I'm sorry to hear that. I'm going to hang up now. I'll pray for you." The line went dead.

Jim rolled another joint. As he pulled the smoke deep into his lungs another plan formed in his mind. He looked for the Savannah telephone book in his bookcase. He was sure he'd brought it with him to Atlanta. He fumbled through the pages. He called the synagogue and asked for the contact information for the president. He wrote the name and number on the palm of his hand. "Do you know that your rabbi is a queer?"

"I beg your pardon. I'm quite sure you must have the wrong number."

Jim almost fell over the footstool at the end of his chair. His words slurred, "No. I'm trying to tell you that your rabbi is a homosexual."

"Really? And how do you know this to be true?"

"Because I've seen him with his lover."

"And why are you telling me this?"

"I'm trying to expose a hypocrite."

"Oh, I suspect your motives are far less pure. What is your name?"

"That's not important."

"It is if I'm to believe you."

"Are you the president of the synagogue?"

"I am. Well, aren't you upset that your rabbi is screwing a Gentile?"

"Any Gentile in particular?"

"Yes, the Bishop of Savannah."

"The Catholic Bishop?"

"No, the Episcopal one."

"Well, I thank you for your call."

"Are you going to fire him?"

"Why would I fire him?"

"You know. Because of what I told you."

"No. As drunk as I think you are, you've actually done me a favor. You see, some of us already suspected what you seem to have confirmed."

"So you're not going to fire him?"

"To the contrary. I don't know who you are, but you have telephoned the wrong person. I'm gay and my partner is a Gentile. We have several gay and lesbian members in our congregation. There is no reason to fire Rabbi Dolan. You have actually given him even more job security. But thanks for your call. I'm going to hang up now. Shalom Aleichem."

Jim Vernon began to sob. "Won't someone help me get even with him? He broke my heart." He fell back on the sofa and cried himself to sleep.

The Magnolia Series

Dennis R. Maynard

"Hey there, handsome."

"Hey yourself."

Bishop Sean Evans squeezed the shoulder of Rabbi Eze Dolan with his hand before seating himself. They were enjoying their daily lunch together in the bar at *The Camellia Hotel*. The hotel was located exactly halfway between the diocesan office and Temple Beth Israel. It was easy walking distance for both. They tried to have lunch together every day that their schedules allowed.

"What would you gentlemen like to drink?"

Sean ordered first. "I'll have my usual. Just bring me a large glass of sweet tea."

Eze ordered next. "I'll have the same."

Sean was surprised. "What? You're having a sweet tea? After all the lectures on the dangers of sugar it appears to me you've come over to the dark side."

"Okay, calm down. I've actually learned to like it. When you're in Rome, do as the Romans do."

Sean shook his head in amusement. "I don't believe it."

"Okay, just claim the victory."

"Do you know what you'd like for lunch?" The waiter asked.

"Do you have any specials?"

"The chef received a fresh shipment of oysters. He can prepare them most any way you'd like."

Eze grinned, "Oysters? Hmm, I think I'd like a dozen on the half shell."

Sean smiled back at him. "Yes, that sounds good. I'll have the same." After the waiter walked away, Sean leaned seductively across the table, "Hmm, are you thinking what I'm thinking?"

Eze winked at him. "It seems to me that after we eat all

those oysters we're going to have to do something to work them off. Are you free to go back to my place after lunch?"

"I think I can swing that."

"Great! As soon as our oysters come, let's eat up."

Sean asked, "How's your morning going?"

"Today is my teaching preparation day so I spent most of it working on my lesson for my Shabbat services this week." Eze started to take a sip from his iced tea and then quickly put the glass back down on the table. "I did have the strangest telephone call."

"Oh?"

"The president of my synagogue called me. He said he wanted to tell me a few personal things about himself. He wanted me to know that he's gay. I can't say I was surprised because I thought he was giving me the gay vibe during my job interviews with him. Anyway, he wanted me to know that he has a life partner. He said only his closest friends in the synagogue know about his lifestyle."

"That's interesting. So basically, he confirmed what you'd suspected about him."

"Here's the interesting part. He wanted me to know that his partner is a Gentile. He's a practicing urologist right here in Savannah. He invited me to come over one evening and have dinner with the two of them."

"Well, that's nice."

"Maybe. Here's the real kicker. He told me that it would be perfectly acceptable if I wanted to bring a date with me."

"Well, that's not all that unusual. You're single. He was probably suggesting that you bring a woman."

"After that preamble, I don't think so. Sean, it was just the tone in his voice and the way he issued the invitation. I think he knows about me, but I think he also knows about you. I think he knows about us."

Sean was silent and sat staring at the plate of oysters the waiter had just placed on the table in front of him. Eze snapped his fingers. "Hello. Are you there?"

"I'd pretty much dismissed it, but Eze, I got a puzzling

telephone call this morning as well."

"Oh? Tell me about it."

"The call came from the rector of the most conservative parish in this diocese. His wife had been in the hospital with a life-threatening illness. I had tried to help them through it. I thought he was just calling to express his appreciation. He did add a little news to the conversation that I didn't know. I hadn't thought much about it until now. He told me that one of his sons is gay. He said that he disapproved of his life choice, but he was his son and he loved him. He concluded the phone call by telling me that I was his bishop. He wanted me to know that he'd always have my back."

"He knows."

"That's what I'm thinking. I just don't know how anyone could find out. We've been so careful."

"Those people from Falls City know."

Sean shook his head. "No, Mister Clemons and Steele Austin and would never betray us. I don't believe it was them."

"There's one more."

Sean nodded, "Jim."

"He's very angry. And I think he's still in love with you."

"Oh, he's angry and bitter, but he's not in love with me. It's just that his pride has been hurt."

"What would you do if our relationship became an issue? It could cost you your ministry."

"I know. I believe with all my heart that God wants me to be a priest. I would hate to have it taken from me. But the same could happen to you. We could be heading into some pretty rough waters."

"Listen, I believe the same God that wants you to be a priest also wants me to be a rabbi. As far as rough waters are concerned, my people have been there before. Don't forget, God let us wander around in the desert for forty years."

"Yes, and it was our guy that calmed the sea."

"Excuse me Father, have you forgotten that he was our guy first?"

After they'd finished laughing at their own verbal duel

Eze asked, "Seriously Sean, what would you do?"

"I know that I'm doing what God wants me to do and I love most every day I show up for work. But Eze, if it comes down to a choice between being a bishop or my love for you, I'll choose you. I believe that God would understand."

Eze then did something they'd never publicly done in Savannah. He reached across the table and took Sean's hand in his. He looked into Sean's eyes and said simply, "I love you. If it comes down to it, I will always choose you as well."

The Magnolia Series

Dennis R. Maynard

CHAPTER

22

"I thought I told them to keep that back door locked. How'd you get in here?" Chief Sparks looked up from his desk to see Stone Clemons standing in the doorway.

"I just followed the smell of that stinky cigar you've got in your mouth. I could smell that thing from the street, and you haven't even lit it."

"I never light it."

"I know. It's your signature. So why do you even have one if you're not going to light it?"

"How long have I known you and how many times have you asked me that same damn question about my cigar? Give it a rest."

Stone shrugged and took a seat opposite the Chief's desk. "I understand you got some results back."

"I do, but first let me tell you a little story. Did you hear about the old fisherman that kept a stick with him when he went fishing?"

"What kind of stick?"

"I'm getting to that. It seems he'd cut a stick to exactly nine inches. Whenever he caught a fish he'd hold it up against that stick. If the fish was longer than the stick he'd throw it back. If it was shorter, he'd keep it."

"That's strange."

"Not really. One day he was asked why he kept the ones that were shorter than his nine-inch stick and threw the bigger ones back. He scoffed, 'Because my frying pan is only nine inches wide.' "

Stone chuckled. "That's a good one."

"Well, this investigation is not unlike that fisherman. We have to be careful not to throw back anything that doesn't match our preconceived ideas. You and I have our suspicions about what happened to the preacher in that house, but we have to prove it. We just might have to be open to some other possibilities."

"I couldn't agree more. So what do you have?"

"Let's do the simple things first. My lab confirms that the red blotches we found on the rector are lipstick. We took photos of them at the hospital and found those lipstick smears in some mighty strange places. We know that doing cardiac resuscitation on the man is not compatible with the location of the blotches."

"Okay, that makes sense."

"The rape kit turned up a long hair located in an equally strange place."

"And the glass I gave you?"

"Thankfully, you did not spill the tea in the glass when you removed it. By the way, how did you remove it?"

"When everyone was occupied with their own concerns, I simply put one of her table napkins around it to preserve the fingerprints and slid it into my coat pocket."

"Remind me to count the silver and crystal after you eat at my house."

"It won't be a problem since you don't have anything worth stealing. Now tell me about the test."

"Have you ever heard of GHB?"

"Sure. It's called the date rate drug."

"Well, the tea tested positive for it as did the preacher's urine sample, blood, and his hair follicle."

"I'll be damned. You mean that woman was trying to rape our priest?"

"Remember the story of the nine-inch frying pan. We can't get ahead of ourselves. We do know that there were two sets of fingerprints on that glass. I don't have Steele's on record, but I do have hers. She's in the system. Her prints are the only ones that matter. We will be able to prove that she handed him the glass."

"Well, is that enough to take to the prosecutor?"

"Like I said, nine-inch frying pan. I've sent the lipstick swabs and the hair strand off for a DNA test. That takes a little longer. I want to seal up as much evidence as possible before taking anything to the prosecutor."

"Sounds good to me."

"There's still one more fish I need to measure."

"What's that?"

"Her story. Walk with me."

"Where we going?"

"To an interrogation room."

When they entered the room Bernice, the Willoughby's maid, was anxiously sitting at the table. "Bernice, I'm Chief Sparks and this is Mister Stone Clemons. MIster Clemons is Father Austin's attorney."

"Yes suh. I knows both you. I saw both you's pictures on the tv."

"Bernice I need to ask you some questions."

"Am I in trouble?"

"Not as long as you tell me the truth. You lie to me or leave out any important detail and you could end up in major trouble."

"Am I under arrest?"

"No, Bernice. You are here because we believe you can shed some light on what happened to Father Austin at the Willoughby house."

"I'sa understand."

"Bernice, were you working that day?"

"Yes suh, I'sa supposed to work that day."

"The entire day?"

"Yes, suh, 'ceptn Miss Virginia gave me the afternoon off."

"Why did she give you the afternoon off? Did you ask for it?"

"No suh."

"Bernice, Mrs. Willoughby told us that you had to leave in order to go over to the school to pick up one of your children that was ill?"

"Did you?"

"No, suh."

"Did Mrs. Willoughby give you a story to use if anyone asked you any questions about that day?"

Bernice began to cry. "Oh, please Mistuh Chief. I'sa don't want to get no one in trouble."

"Just tell us the truth. It's very important. Were you there when Father Austin arrived?"

"Yes suh. MIss Virginia tells me to answer the door whens he rings. I shows him to 'da library. Just as she say, I tell him she be right with him."

"Then what?"

"I'sa don't know. That's when I left."

"Was Mister Willoughby at home?"

"No suh, he up in Augusta play'n golf."

"When did he get home?"

"I don't know nothin' 'bout that."

"Okay, Bernice you can go."

"Does Miss Virginia knows I be talk'n to you all?"

"No."

"I'sa so 'fraid she gonna fire me."

"Bernice, I don't have any control over that, but if I were you, I'd tell Mister Willoughby everything you've told us."

"I'sa already has."

"You've told Mister Willoughby all this?"

"Yes suh. I already did."

"Bernice, I think your job is secure."

"Can I go now?"

"I'll have one of my officers drive you home."

Stone tapped the table. "So what's next?"

"We wait on the DNA tests."

"Do you need to wait until they get back to tell Steele and Randi what we've learned?"

The Chief frowned. "If I can get you to agree, I think we should. Let's make sure all the fish fit in the pan before we tell him."

"You realize this whole thing could blow up in our face. I can see all the headlines now, *Episcopal Priest Raped By Female Member of His Church.*"

"Well, that's exactly why I asked you to be here. I need you to help me figure a way to keep all that from happening. It wouldn't be good for Steele and Randi, and it sure wouldn't be good for First Church. We've got to figure out a way to make her pay for what we think she tried to do. We have to do so without it becoming the lead story in all the cheap newspapers and magazines."

Stone scowled. Clearly the wheels had already begun to turn in his head. "You got another one of those cigars?"

"I didn't know you smoked."

"I don't. I'm just going to chew on it. It might help me think."

The Magnolia Series

Dennis R. Maynard

CHAPTER

23

"Ladies, please come in. May I offer you a glass of champagne?" Almeda, Rose, and Rose's daughter had just walked into *Lydia's Boutique* in the exclusive Buckhead area of Atlanta. They were there to shop for a wedding dress for Rose and a dress for her daughter to wear for the wedding.

The attendant asked Rose's daughter, "And what would you like to drink?"

"Do you have a *Co-Cola*?"

"Aren't you just the cutest thing? Of course we do. This is Atlanta."

The attendant led them to a sofa before a carpeted platform. A man wearing a tuxedo and white gloves brought them their drinks on a silver tray. "Almeda," Rose whispered. "The clothes here must be awfully expensive."

Almeda smiled. "That's not your concern. We are here to find you both beautiful dresses to wear on your special day. We might also see something that I might like to wear as well."

Almeda had arranged this two-day adventure. She'd hired a stretch limousine to carry Rose and her children to Atlanta, along with Horace and herself. While she was shopping with the girls, Horace would take the boys to purchase suitable *Morning Coats* to wear for the noon wedding. At first, Rose had protested. "We don't need to buy the boys formal wear. They'll just outgrow them. We can rent something."

Almeda was aghast. "Rose, you can't be serious. You have no idea who could have worn a rented suit before them. The very thought." Almeda put her hand over her heart and drew in a deep breath. "Rented clothing could contain bedbugs or lice or God only knows what. No. I'll not hear of it." Rose knew better than to argue.

"We're going to stay at this cute little hotel that I own in Buckhead."

Rose couldn't help but express her surprise. "Almeda, you own a hotel in Atlanta? I had no idea."

Almeda shushed her. "Oh that, I didn't know I owned it either until I met with my financial advisor a couple of weeks ago. Chadsworth, my first husband, had the golden touch when it came to investing and making money. Every time I have a meeting with my investment counselor he reviews my investments with me. If I didn't know better I'd think that Chadsworth was still alive and overseeing my finances."

Rose was actually able to choose the dresses she wanted for herself and her daughter. She protested the price. "Almeda, this dress is more than I paid for my car after Melvin left."

"If those are the dresses you want, then those are the dresses you shall have. Now what do you think of the one I've chosen for myself?"

Rose couldn't wait to show Elmer. She was pleased with the way the dress looked on her, but she still had some qualms about the cost.

After Horace and the boys rejoined them they were driven to *Stone Mountain*. The centerpiece of this amusement park is an enormous rock relief on the side of the mountain. It depicts three heroic Confederate generals and their respective horses. The sculptures of Generals Jefferson Davis, Robert E. Lee, and Stonewall Jackson are the most visited attraction in the entire State of Georgia. But it is not without controversy. It is the site of the founding of the 1915 edition of the *Ku Klux Klan*.

Almeda did not bring the MacClaren children here for controversy but for amusement. There was a full day and evening list of activities they could enjoy. "Here is a map of all the attractions. Go and have fun. Then meet me at this very spot by our limousine at 6:00 p.m. We'll have a picnic here at the foot of the memorial and watch the laser light show tonight."

Almeda had instructed the limousine chauffer to pick up the basket she ordered for their picnic. She had ordered from a little family owned bakery that was well known in Georgia for their fresh baked croissants. Her driver was to pick up chicken croissant sandwiches, homemade sweet potato chips, and Italian coleslaw made with rice vinegar. She'd also ordered a couple of bottles of *Rombauer Chardonnay*, sodas, and bottles of *Evian Water*. Dessert was to be an assortment of *French Fruit Tarts*.

As they were eating, Rose couldn't help but ask Horace a question that was bothering her. "Horace, I don't want to offend you, but there's something I'd really like to ask you."

"Okay. I assure you I can't imagine any question you could ask me would be offensive."

"You don't have to answer me. I'll understand."

"Please, ask your question."

"Horace, you're an African American."

Horace chuckled, "I am? When did that happen?" Horace pulled his shirtsleeves up. "My God, I'm black. Too much sun I guess." He continued to laugh.

Rose smiled, "Oh, just forget it."

"No, please. I was only having some fun with you. Ask your question."

"Okay. As an African American, what do you think, no, what do you feel looking up at that sculpture?"

"Frankly, I'm a bit overwhelmed by it. I can't imagine the artistic ingenuity that created anything that large. I read that carving takes up over an acre and half on the side of that mountain. At it's deepest point it goes twelve feet into the mountain. That is an engineering and artistic masterpiece."

"But I've read that there have been calls to have it removed."

"I know its history is not pure. I know that what it represents is upsetting for some people of color. You see, Rose, I'm not from the South. My last home was up in Washington, D.C. I married a Southern woman. I've learned to appreciate many things about the South. I don't think

Almeda has a prejudiced bone in her body. My God, she's married to a black man. I don't think that when she looks up at that mountain she sees racism. I think she sees military leaders that made a significant contribution to the history of this country."

"But they fought to maintain slavery."

"I understand that. But what is gained by re-fighting a war that ended over one hundred years ago? Rose, do I wish that carving up there had never been made? Probably so, but there it is. Will we be able to go back and undo slavery by getting rid of it? Of course not, so why not appreciate it for what it is. It's a reminder of a time in this nation when brother turned against brother. It's a symbol of a time when this nation was on the verge of being ripped asunder. White men and black men fought side by side to insure the American dream could be made possible for every man and woman regardless of skin color.

You see, I'm not for taking down all the confederate monuments. That accomplishes absolutely nothing and in the long run may prove to be the wrong thing to do. I want them to be retained. I don't see them honoring bad behavior. I see them as a reminder of a time in our history that we survived and that we never want to repeat. Removing them will not change the past. Keeping them reminds us of a past we never want to bring into the present. Monuments like this one remind us that it's a past we never want to repeat. Have you ever been to Europe?"

"No."

"When you go I hope you'll visit some of the great cathedrals. Please notice that many of the stained glass windows are damaged along with much of the statuary. That was done hundreds of years ago. The Puritans tried to erase any symbol they thought was Roman Catholic. The Anglican and Catholic Churches could have repaired that damage or simply replaced the windows and statues. They've chosen not to. We need to remember.

If you go to Germany you can visit the death camps like

Auschwitz. The despicable gas chambers and ovens are still standing. You would think that they should have been bulldozed and wiped from the face of the earth. They still stand because we need to remember.

In Berlin there is a Nazi Museum. We usually think of museums as places of education. That one is. We must not forget.

Or let's go even further back. Let's go to Rome. The remains of the Coliseum still stand. Tourists flock to it. It's an architectural masterpiece. By all rights, it too should have been demolished. On the floor of that coliseum Christian men, women, and children were massacred and fed to the lions for the crowd's entertainment. Why would we try to preserve such an ugly piece of history? We must not forget. Does that help you?"

Rose nodded, "Thank you. I believe I now understand how you're able to sit here drinking chardonnay and chatting at the foot of a Confederate Memorial."

"But Rose, I don't see it as a Confederate Memorial. I see it as a historical reminder. It points to some very dark days in our American history; it's a part of our American story that we must not forget. If this country is going to have a secure future it must not try to rewrite its history. We must record our history accurately. That monument on the side of that mountain is a part of that history. Those generals fought for what they believed in. Theirs was a cause I despise. I need them to be on the side of the mountain to remind me of that. Hopefully, it will remind every citizen in this freedom-loving America. Removing it removes one more reminder we can't afford to lose.

Trying to pretend that this nation was never divided on that issue accomplishes nothing. We need to remember. We must not forget. The very future of this nation depends on it. Those who forget their pasts are destined to relive them. We can remove every monument and Confederate statue in this nation. We can eradicate them from the face of the earth, but what will we have accomplished? Removing them does not convert a single bigot. Only God can change the hearts of men and women. Only God can remove the bigotry, hatred, and racism. Removing statues like the one that's on the side of that mountain doesn't change a single heart. Leave them alone. Let them remind us of who we once were, but not who we are now, or who we will become. Removing all the statues will not change any person's belief. We need God to do that."

Just then the sky exploded with fireworks as the laser light show began. The sound system blared Ray Charles singing, *Georgia On My Mind*.

The Magnolia Series

Dennis R. Maynard

24

Virginia Mudd Willoughby's anxiety level had reached the point of panic. She had searched the library for the glass she'd given Father Austin with the GHB in it. It was nowhere to be found.

Something was going on with Thackston. Outwardly he treated her just as he always had. It was the way he looked at her that had changed. When she tried to talk to him about anything she felt like he was interviewing her. He asked her questions about the smallest detail every time she tried to talk to him. She had the feeling he didn't believe her. Then she reassured herself. Thackston had only asked her about the events surrounding Father Austin one time. Since then he'd not even brought it up.

He did not kiss her in the same way either. When she tried to prolong a kiss or an embrace he pulled away. He seemed content with what she could best describe as a peck. Before the event with the priest, Thackston's kisses and embraces lingered. Still, she wanted to believe that he loved her.

Even their lovemaking had changed. In the past he smothered her body with affection. Now that intimacy was missing. It had become something else. His approach lacked love. It was as though he wanted their time together to be over as quickly as possible. He hadn't initiated making love to her since that event. It was always her idea.

Virginia remembered that Thackston used to tell her several times each day that he loved her. He never went to sleep at night without telling her. Now he only told her in response to her own expression. But it was so perfunctory. She thought his words sounded more like the words in a stage play.

She was desperate to believe that her husband couldn't

possibly know that she'd tried to take advantage of Father Austin. There's no way he could. She felt as though her cover story had been a good one. In fact, she thought it was rather clever. She knew the doctors would find no evidence of a heart attack. Still, she commended herself for coming up with the story so quickly.

As for the GHB, the bartender she bought it from had assured her that it was not detectable. She tried to convince herself that she had nothing to worry about.

Maybe Thackston's behavior has nothing to do with her. He does have a big case coming up for trial. She knew that could explain his behavior. He was simply preoccupied with that. She would feel better if she could just find that missing glass.

Then there was Bernice. She was unable to make eye contact with her. She'd asked her directly if anyone had asked her about her whereabouts on the day Father Austin had his heart attack. She'd assured her they hadn't. It was the tone in her voice that led Virginia to be suspicious. She was definitely acting different. But when it came right down to it, Virginia knew she had the advantage. Given a choice between believing his wife and the maid, her husband would believe her. Even if the police were to question Bernice, her credibility as a black maid would be dubious.

Virginia continually rehearsed all this in her mind when she tried to fall asleep at night. Often the fears would overwhelm her during the day. She would go through every detail again and then finally reassure herself she had nothing to be anxious about.

In the interim, Virginia needed to resume her role as the perfect Southern housewife. She'd done it before. She was thinking about some of the rules that every Southern woman had drilled into them from an early age. Virginia smiled to herself as she remembered them. Always write *thank you notes* immediately. Cross your legs at the ankles. Liberally use the words *ma'am* and *sir* in conversation. Make sure your guests never leave your home hungry. And, of course, never serve day-old sweet tea.

Virginia was thinking of the rules her *Mothah* had drilled into her. Every Southern *Mothah* made sure that a proper daughter of theirs knew these rules. They were reinforced before their wedding night. And at the slightest hint of trouble in the marriage, a daughter could count on having their *Mothah* question if they were adhering to the rules.

The rules were simple enough but did require effort. A dutiful Southern wife always made certain that she rose before her husband. She would bathe and put on her makeup. She'd brush her hair and style it for the day. She then dressed and put on her heels. A Southern lady never let her husband greet her wearing pajamas, a house robe, and slippers. The only time it's appropriate for a husband to see his wife in sleepwear is if it's sheer and designed for seduction.

Once she was dressed, she would quietly go to the kitchen to insure *The Help* had his breakfast prepared. She would check the table to make sure that it was set properly. It was also important to see that his morning newspaper was folded and placed on the table next to his plate. Once all was in readiness, she could return to the master suite. While he was showering and getting dressed she would make the bed. A Southern lady always made the bed as soon as possible in the morning.

After sharing breakfast with her husband, a good wife would walk him to the door and give him a hug and kiss that would make him anxious to return home to her.

When he arrives home from work she'll be waiting for him with his favorite cocktail in hand. And when it came to bedtime, a Southern lady went to bed with her husband prepared to satisfy his needs. Her nightly ritual of face cream was never applied until after he'd gone to sleep. Her *Mothah* had drilled that into her. No proper wife ever allowed her husband to see her without her makeup and properly coiffed hair.

Virginia had been very careful to follow all these rules. She did not want Thackston to have any reason not to trust her. She definitely needed him to believe her. Since the event with Father Austin, Virginia had played the role of the perfect wife with military precision.

So far her plan seemed to be working. Virginia had been successful in convincing herself that her anxiety was simply the result of some misplaced religious guilt. With each passing day, the event became less and less worrisome.

Occasionally, her mind reflected back to Steele Austin's naked chest. She touched her own lips, remembering just how soft and kissable his were. She regretted not being able to feel all of him. But those erotic thoughts only resurrected her anxiety, so she dared not linger on them.

With each passing day, Virginia reassured herself the event involving Father Austin was now behind her. Thackston believed her and she'd heard nothing from the police or Father Austin. She relaxed into her daily routine. Virginia surmised she only needed to continue to demonstrate to her husband that she was nothing but a loving and faithful wife.

Virginia believed that at long last her life was returning to normal. Then at breakfast this morning Thackston asked her, "Virginia, I'm quite curious. What were you going to serve Father Austin for lunch when he came over?"

Her anxiety returned.

The Magnolia Series

Dennis R. Maynard

25

"This check has a lot of zeros on it." Rose was anxious to share her good news with Elmer. "I never thought he'd honor our agreement." Rose had just received a check from her ex-husband, The Reverend Melvin MacClaren. The court-ordered payment was for past child support plus interest. Because Melvin resided in a foreign country, the court also ordered him to forward pay all the child support due until John Calvin achieved the age of eighteen.

"It doesn't sound to me like he had any choice. I'm just amazed at how quickly the Family Court acted."

"I think it had more to do with Stone Clemons and his law firm than it did with the efficiency of the Family Court. He asked the court to confiscate Melvin's passport if he refused to pay."

"That sounds like something Stone Clemons would do. I'm just happy they were able to make him pay up."

"I'm still in a state of shock. I really didn't think he'd pay any child support."

"What are you going to do with the money?"

"Elmer, I'd like to pay Almeda back for all the wonderful things she's done for us."

"Honey, you'd better clear that idea with your attorney. I'm not a lawyer, but I think child support payments have to be used for your children. I believe it's a violation of the law to use that money for any other purpose. Besides, I don't think Almeda would let you reimburse her. She loves you and she loves our children. That's the one and only reason she's been so generous with you."

"I just wish I could do something for her."

"Have you ever heard the expression *generous givers must also learn how to be gracious receivers?*"

"I suppose you're right. But Elmer, I would really like to

do something for her."

"You can. Just let her love you and then love her back. Honestly, more money is the last thing she needs. She does need a genuine friend that is devoted to her with a pure motive. I've known her a long time. Everyone in this town gives her respect and deference, but it's not out of friendship. They do so because of her wealth and social position. If the truth could be told, many people tip their hat to her out of fear. They're actually afraid of her. I'm not sure she's ever had a real friend. You can be a true friend. That's the greatest gift she'll ever receive in this life."

"Don't you think Doctor Drummond is her friend?"

"Of course, but he's her husband. I think he worships the ground she walks on. Rose, Honey, you may be the first person other than family that can freely offer her love and friendship."

"I guess I never thought of her as being friendless."

"I could be wrong, but I think she's probably a very lonely person. That's why she stays so busy trying to control the world. She needs to be in complete charge of everything that happens in Falls City society and First Church."

"You may be right. I do enjoy her company. We have great fun together."

"Speaking of that, how was your Atlanta shopping trip?"

"It was wonderful. She hired a limousine, kept us in the nicest hotel, and then we had an incredible evening at *Stone Mountain*. The children were ecstatic."

"Did you find a dress?"

"I did, but Almeda tells me you don't get to see it until our wedding."

"I can't wait."

"The boys look so handsome in their *Morning Coats*. Almeda insisted on buying them. She has some pretty strong opinions about renting formal wear."

Elmer chuckled. "Imagine that."

"Honey, I suppose you can rent yours. You don't have to buy one to wear just one time. She'll never know." That comment really struck Elmer as funny. Rose interrupted his laughter. "Just what's so funny about that?"

"Rose, I grew up in Southern society. Every Southern gentleman worth his salt has three pieces of formal wear in his closet. I have all three. I have tails, pants, and white gloves for those occasions when *White Tie* is mandated. I have a tuxedo to wear when the invitation dictates *Black Tie*. And I have a *Morning Coat* and all the trimmings for formal daytime events."

"And how often do you wear any of those?"

"There are few daytime formal events so my *Morning Coat* has not received much exercise. There are usually two or three *White Tie* events a year. Or at least, when I was married to Judith there were. She was more interested in the *White Tie* events than I was. My tuxedo used to get quite a workout. There are many more *Black Tie* events. At First Church, guests are expected to wear *Black Tie* at evening weddings when the invitation notes it."

"Really?"

"You'll see. As we become more active at First Church the invitations will get more plentiful. And if you and Almeda continue as best friends, she's going to make sure that we are included in all the upper-crust social events."

"It sounds curious, exciting, and terrifying at the same time."

"Honey, take it from someone who has been there and done that. After a while it will get tiresome. You'll begin to ask yourself just why all these people keep getting dressed up in uncomfortable clothes. The ultimate question is why are they pretending to be important when the rest of the world couldn't care less."

"Have you had a chance to talk to Almeda about the food for our reception?"

"I thought maybe we'd get to do that on the trip up to Atlanta, but she said she wasn't ready. But she did promise that we'd discuss it soon."

"I promise you that whatever Almeda undertakes will be

done well and no one will complain."

"I know you're right. For now, I just want to enjoy being in love with you."

"Thanks for saying that. I love you too."

"Elmer, can I put this check in an investment account and save it for the kid's college educations?"

"I'd ask your attorney before I did anything with it. If he does say you can put it in a savings account, I'd ask your new best friend for investment advice."

"Wait! Elmer, how long has it been since you wore any of that formal wear in your closet?"

"I don't know. It's been awhile. Why?"

"Did you buy all those clothes before you lost weight?"

The Magnolia Series

Dennis R. Maynard

26

Steele Austin had just returned from lunch. When he entered his office, his secretary, Crystal, greeted him. "Father Austin, you have an urgent telephone call." She handed him a pink call sheet. Steele glanced at it. "He says he wants you to call him on a secure line."

Steele nodded and whispered, "Crystal, please get your telephone call pad."

Crystal returned with the pink telephone message pad. Steele tore off the top carbon copy of the phone call she had just handed him. He ripped it into several pieces and then placed it in the ashtray on his desk. He lit a match and burned it. Crystal's eyes grew large. "What are you doing?"

"Crystal, this is a highly sensitive telephone call. I want no record of it."

"So you know Earle LaFitte?"

"Crystal, it's imperative that you forget his name and this phone call. Do you understand?"

"If you say so. But Father Austin, even if you call him on your private line there will be a record of the call."

"You're right. Where are the closest public telephone booths?"

Crystal thought for a minute. "I don't think they have any booths, but I have seen public phones off the lobby at the *Hyatt.*"

The *Hyatt Regency* was a short walk from First Church. "Great, I'll be back in a few minutes."

When Steele arrived at the *Hyatt* he dialed the number on the pink slip. "Steele, is that you?"

"Chadsworth, where are you?"

"I'm staying at the *Hyatt* in Falls City."

"Chadsworth, I'm in the lobby."

"How did you know I was here?"

"I didn't. I came here to call you on a secure line."

"Come up to room 825."

Steele knocked on the door. When Chadsworth opened it, Steele almost didn't recognize him. Chadsworth had lost weight that he could ill afford to lose. He looked haggard and distraught. Steele thought he'd been crying. He opened his arms and hugged him. "Please come in before someone sees us."

Chadsworth led him to a sitting area in the room. "Do you want a drink?"

"No, I don't need anything, but thanks. Chadsworth, what's going on? You're taking a big risk coming back to Falls City."

"I know. I came in on a private plane. I wore a disguise to the hotel. No one knows I'm here. Steele, I just have to talk to you in person. I need your help."

Chadsworth had been married to Almeda at one time. He'd lived a double life. He was a respectable husband and businessman in Falls City. When he could, he traveled to Atlanta to be with his lover, Earle LaFitte. When Earle contracted AIDS and died, Chadsworth faked his own suicide. He used Earle's death as a way to gain his freedom. He moved to San Francisco where he could live into his identity. He continued to care for Almeda through a trust he'd left her. He'd also given Steele management over an endowment fund at First Church. Earle's ashes are buried in the First Church Cemetery. The grave marker records it as the burial place of Chadsworth Purcell Alexander.

Chadsworth began to cry. "Steele, I really need you."

"I'm here for you." Steele took Chadworth's hand and squeezed it. "You're in a safe place. Talk to me."

"Steele, Eric is cheating on me!" Chadsworth began to sob. "We got married. I don't know if you knew that. We've been together for almost twenty years. He even wanted to change his name from Eric Schneider to Eric Alexander. I thought we were going to be together forever. Then he did this." More tears flowed from Chadsworth's eyes.

"Are you sure? How do you know?"

"There were so many signs. I tried to ignore all of them. There were whispered phone calls. There were the times that he pretended to be talking to a friend. Everything in me told me that he wasn't talking to an acquaintance. He lost a lot of weight and got really cut. Isn't that the first thing every cheating spouse does? They all lose weight. Suddenly he became concerned about his breath. He was buying all kinds of breath mints and chewing gum. Then I found a little vile of edible lubricant in his gym bag. It was a flavor and texture we'd never used together. He bought some new clothes and changed his hairstyle. He even got some Botox injections. God, I was just so stupid not to see it."

"Chadsworth, I'm really sorry."

"Then I found a pre-paid telephone card. You know the kind that you can use to make calls but the call doesn't show up on your telephone bill?"

"I've never used one, but I know they exist."

"I guess the most telling of all was when he started talking about his new best friend in another city that I'd never heard of before. He would talk to this new friend on the phone at some of the strangest times day and night."

"I think the final piece was when he told me he needed to go back to his home town in order to check on things."

"All of those are pretty suspicious. Are you positive that there's someone else?"

"I am now." Chadsworth opened a briefcase that was lying on the table in front of them. He tossed some photos to Steele. Steele glanced at them. They clearly proved that Eric was having sex with a man half his age. "I simply had to know the truth. So I hired a private detective. The only spouse that doesn't have to know is the one that doesn't want to know. I did."

"Have you confronted him?"

"Yes. I've gotten all the same bullshit lines any cheating spouse might offer. 'I'm so sorry. Don't you think our love can see us through this? I didn't know what I was doing. It was only sex.' You know the excuses as well as I do."

"Do you still love him?"

"Yes, damn it. That's why it hurts so much."

"Can you forgive him?"

"He's wants me to. He's made all the right promises. He promises never to do it again."

"Do you believe him?"

"I don't know. Is he contrite because he's truly sorry or is he contrite because he got caught?"

"You're the only person that can answer that question. Where is he now?"

"He's at our place in San Francisco. I've not kicked him out yet, but I'm considering it."

"Do you want to forgive him?"

"I think so. I don't know if I will ever be able to trust him again."

"Chadsworth, I'm sorry to tell you that I don't think you ever will. This is what I've learned from others in your same situation. You will never be able to completely trust a cheating spouse again. Every time they are out of your sight you're going to wonder if they're cheating on you. Every phone call and every suspicious note or card that comes in the mail will leave you questioning their fidelity. I'm not going to lie to you. I think the happier spouse is the one that divorces the cheater. But if you're willing to live with the doubts for the rest of your marriage, then you need to forgive him and move on with your life together."

"But Steele, I really love him."

"And that's what makes your decision so difficult. But only you can decide."

The Magnolia Series

Dennis R. Maynard

CHAPTER

27

"Father, Mister Mitchell is here. He has an appointment. He's in the waiting room."

Steele drew in a deep breath. "Thanks, show him in."

Colonel Mitchell walked into Steele's office carrying a thick manila folder. He walked directly to Steele's couch and seated himself. "And a very good morning to you too, Colonel," Steele chuckled. "Please have a seat."

Steele sat in one of his wingback chairs opposite the couch. "Tell me why you have honored me with this visit."

"There! Right there!" Colonel Mitchell's voice reeked with disgust. "That's your problem."

"You're going to have to be more specific."

"It's your arrogance. You think you're so damn cute. Well, I'm here to tell you that you're not. And look at the way you're sitting in that chair. You're all sunk in like you don't have a care in the world."

"And just how would you prefer me to sit?"

"Can you even spell the word humility?"

"Do I understand that it's your contention that I'm sitting in an arrogant manner?"

"Exactly. That's nothing but a chair. It's not your royal throne."

Steele stood and reseated himself. He crossed his legs. He couldn't disguise his amusement. "Tell me now, is that more humble?"

"You're hopeless."

"Mister Mitchell, you've not done anything to hide your dislike for me from the day I arrived. I'm not sure what I did to deserve your distaste. I believe I've always treated you with courtesy and respect. I'm just sorry that it's not been returned."

"Respect is earned. You've earned none of mine."

"Just what is it about me you find so irritating?"

"I just told you. You're arrogant. Priests are supposed to be humble. You're filled with pride."

"Wow. Is that all?"

"You're not very spiritual. Priests are spiritual. There is nothing spiritual about you."

"Gosh, if I thought those were accurate descriptions of me, I wouldn't care much for me either."

Colonel Mitchell raised his voice. "Do you think that was funny?"

Steele felt his patience running thin. "Okay, I no longer find dissecting my shortcomings to be a recreational activity. Why are you here?"

"There you go again. You really are quite disgusting."

Steele stood. "Sir, this visit is over." He started walking toward his door.

"I'm not leaving without giving you this." He handed Steele the manila folder. "It's a petition signed by over two hundred of your members. It demands that you and the vestry cut the giving to the diocese by fifty percent. It states that none of the funds given to First Church will ever go to the National Episcopal Church."

"On what grounds would we decrease our support for the missions in this diocese? And why on earth would we cease to support the National Church?"

"For all the reasons we outlined for you at the last vestry meeting. The Episcopal Church has fallen into multiple heresies. And you've led this congregation right down that same heretical highway."

"You realize that not everyone agrees with you."

"The people that matter do."

"Colonel, I'd like to think everyone matters whether they agree with me or not."

Colonel spit the next words out of his mouth. "How can any Christian support gay marriage, female priests, and baby killing? You're a priest. You should know better."

"Well, according to you, I'm not much of a priest."

"You're right about that. If I ever needed a priest, you'd

be the very last one in the world I'd ever ask to help me."

Steele sat back down. "Colonel, aren't you tired?"

"I sleep perfectly well at night."

"I'm not referencing your sleeping habits. I'm asking you if you haven't grown tired of being angry. Maintaining the level of anger you've exhibited must be exhausting. And all the anger and displeasure that you have toward me must drain you."

"I'm not tired and my anger is justified."

"Colonel, I don't think I will ever be able to do anything to earn your favor. You don't like me and I have to confess that feeling has grown to be mutual. But we're different. I think I live in your head twenty-four hours a day seven days a week. I regret to inform you that you do not live in mine."

"There is something you could do to help both of us."

"Oh, pray tell?"

"You are the rector of one of the largest parishes in this nation. You could take a public stand against all the heresies The Episcopal Church has fallen into. You could condemn every one of them. Your voice would be heard. You're just too afraid of offending your big liberal donors to do it."

"Colonel, the National Church has already decided all the things that bother you. They're not going to be undone."

"It's just so sad."

"What is?"

"I just wish we could go back to being the church we were before you came here and destroyed us."

"Please tell me how I destroyed First Church."

"This church used to be a place where proper ladies and gentlemen could worship together. Now there are all kinds of people showing up and acting like they belong."

"But don't you want a church that welcomes everyone?"

"There are other churches the riff raff can attend."

"And you really believe that?"

"I do."

"If you'd just take a stand against female priestesses and queers, you'd see that the less desirable members would leave."

"Is that the real reason you want me to do that? You think it would get rid of some of our current members?"

"Let's just call that a fringe benefit if you will do the right thing."

"Colonel, I don't have a time machine. I can't go back in time and restore First Church to the way it was before I came."

"If you'd leave we could get a rector that would."

"First, I'm not going anywhere. And second, this is an Episcopal Church. First Church will never be anything but an Episcopal Church. That is who we are. It is who we have always been. We are Episcopal Christians."

"Then I feel sorry for you and the Episcopal Church."

"Is there anything else I can do for you?"

"No, obviously you're not going to do the right thing." He stared out the window at First Church, visible from Steele's office window. He shook his head. "Do you know that I was baptized in that building?"

"No, I don't think I did know that."

"I've been a member here my entire life. I was confirmed and married here. I have family members buried out there in the cemetery. I have graves for my wife and me just beyond your windows. I never thought I'd see the day that I no longer felt like this was my church. You and the leaders of this church are displacing people like me. You are leaving us homeless. We don't belong in the Episcopal Church that we've loved all our lives. So Father Austin, just where are we supposed to go?"

Steele winced. "Believe it or not, I really do feel your pain. It even helps me understand some of your anger with the National Church and me. I'm not sure there's much I can say to reassure you. As I said, The Episcopal Church is not going to return to some day in its romantic past."

A tear dropped down Colonel Mitchell's cheek. It stirred a feeling of pity in Steele for the man. He was stuck in the past. The Church had moved into the future and left him behind. Steele asked, "Colonel, would you like me to pray with you?"

Colonel Mitchell stood and shook his head. "I'm sure I need prayer, but as I said earlier you'd be the last priest on the face of the earth I'd want to pray with me." He turned his back on Steele and opened the door.

The Magnolia Series

Dennis R. Maynard

CHAPTER

28

Almeda Alexander Drummond had not been able to sleep through the night for over a week. The day for Rose and Elmer's wedding was fast approaching. She'd volunteered to host their wedding reception in her home. It simply had to measure up to her superior standards. She not only wanted people to attend and enjoy themselves, she wanted to insure that it would be the talk of the town for weeks to come, if not longer.

"Mary Alice, I'm so thankful that you're here. We have so much to do. Martha, I'm surprised to see you." Martha Dexter came through Almeda's door right behind Mary Alice Smythe.

Mary Alice rolled her eyes at Almeda. "She insisted on coming along. Just know that I'm happy to help."

"Mary Alice said you were going to be planning the menu for Rose MacClaren's wedding reception." Martha did not even attempt to contain her anticipation. "Are we going to be sampling items on the menu?"

Almeda shot Mary Alice a knowing look. Mary Alice nodded. "I told you, Martha, we weren't going to be eating. We're just planning the table situation and which foods are to go where."

Martha looked disappointed. "Almeda, I'm thirsty. Do you have any of that delicious lemonade that you served at the bazaar?"

"I have some sweet tea. I'll be happy to get you some of that."

Once again Martha's face flushed with disappointment. Her taste buds were all set for that special lemonade Almeda had served at the church bazaar.

"Mary Alice, we are going to have to draw on your excellent eye for detail to make sure that the staging for the reception is done without error." Mary Alice had been director of the First Church Altar Guild for as long as anyone could remember. It appeared she was going to be the director long past her own demise. Almeda knew that Mary Alice Smythe's attention to detail was beyond dispute.

"Did Colonel Mitchell ask you to sign his petition?"

"What are you talking about?" Almeda was leading her to her backyard and pool area. Martha Dexter followed along behind, slurping the remainder of the tea in her glass before asking Almeda for another glass. Almeda tried not to show just how annoyed she was by Martha's intrusion.

Mary Alice continued. "He's circulating a petition asking the rector and vestry to cut our support to the diocese in half and give nothing to the National Church."

"Oh, that man is always stirring up trouble. He knows better than to ask me to sign it. I'd give him a piece of my mind. I may do so anyway. I hope you didn't sign it."

"Of course I didn't. He's just so angry."

"Let's forget about him. We have a reception to plan."

Once they were standing by her pool, Almeda asked Mary Alice to imagine the scene. "I've ordered a large white tent that will begin here. When the guests exit the solarium they will walk directly into the tent. It will stretch over the pool and go about twenty feet on either side of the pool. It will extend another forty feet beyond the pool itself."

"My goodness, Almeda, that's a huge tent."

"None of the catering services here in Falls City could accommodate me so I'm getting it from a service in Atlanta."

"How many bar stations do you want?"

"I don't want people standing in line for any of the stations. I also don't want them bumping into each other with their drinks or food. That is the number one rule when it comes to Southern etiquette at one of these affairs. Guests must have plenty of room to move about without bumping into one another accidentally. So let's spread the stations out."

"I'll need to think about it, but my first thought is to place a full service bar at each of the four corners of the swimming pool."

"But won't everyone stop at the first one they see?"

"That's certainly a possibility. What if we put the two bars at the far end of the pool on elevated platforms? We can accent them with special lighting."

"That's genius."   Almeda nodded, "Mary Alice, that's the very reason you're here."

"Will you be serving the lemonade that you served at the bazaar?" Martha Dexter asked anxiously.

"No," Almeda exhaled. "There will be a full bar."

"Now let me tell you what I have in mind for the food stations."

"Okay, but let's begin with the centerpiece. I think the wedding cake should be placed right here at the entrance. It will be the first thing that guests see when they exit the solarium and enter the tent. The cutting of the cake will be the last thing the bride and groom do before they leave for their honeymoon. They will be perfectly situated for their exit. Are you going to have a groom's cake?"

Almeda was shocked, "Mary Alice, you certainly know me better than to think I'd have a tacky groom's cake at one of my wedding receptions. Groom's cakes belong at redneck weddings in the country and tacky Yankee weddings."

"I didn't think you would, but I needed to ask."

"Do you think you could get a refrigerated table that we can cover with a tablecloth and place the wedding cake on?"

"Mary Alice, what are you thinking?"

"I'm thinking that one of the most unforgivable breaches of etiquette is to allow the frosting on the wedding cake to melt and begin to run. The refrigerated table will maintain the icing."

"Oh, Mary Alice, you do have an eye for detail."

"Tell me about the food."

"I've talked to Rose about the menu. We've agreed that we don't want it to be a sit down affair. We want people to be able to mingle. We'll need to make provision for the orchestra and a dance floor at the far end of the tent. As for the fare, we've chosen to do finger foods compatible with our Southern heritage. Of course, we'll provide small cocktail plates, forks, and napkins at each food station. We believe that four food stations will be adequate."

"Is one of them to include an ice sculpture?"

"Yes, we thought that the ice sculpture could be surrounded by a large bowl of crushed ice containing shrimp and cocktail sauce. People can place a few shrimp on their plates and then go to another food station. Or they can stand there and eat what they want before moving on."

"The sculpture and shrimp should be placed on a round table so people can access it from all sides."

"I agree."

"On the table with the finger sandwiches we planned on having pulled pork sliders, rosemary biscuits and country ham, cucumber, salmon, and watercress sandwiches, and of course pimento cheese sandwiches. All of them will be bite size."

"That sounds nice."

"We decided on placing deviled eggs, okra and green tomato fritters, stuffed mushrooms, and bacon pimento fritters on the third."

Martha Dexter whined, "I'm getting hungry just hearing the menu. Don't you have samples of any of the food you're going to serve?"

Almeda chose to ignore her. "There will only be one carving station. I'll have a chef carving brisket and placing the slices on the corn pone with some melted cheese. That chef will also be serving the okra beignets. That way he can keep them warm under the heat lamp. As you are well aware, okra beignets simply must be served warm. I've instructed him to serve them with cilantro sour cream sauce."

"That all sounds wonderful. Have you thought about decorations?"

"I have chosen some chandeliers to hang from the tent ceiling, but beyond that I'd like for us to go to the florist and work with them on the floral arrangements."

"I'll work with your set-up crew to make sure that none of the stations are too close to one another."

"Did Rose choose a color for her decorative theme?"

Almeda expelled a deep breath. "Yes, poor thing just doesn't understand all our ways yet. She wants to decorate in red."

"Oh my. That does take the breath away."

"We're really going to have to struggle to keep it from looking tacky."

"Why red?"

"Because her name is Rose."

"Hmm, do you think we could convince her to simply decorate with roses of various colors?"

"Mary Alice, that's a wonderful idea. That way we can make the decor less harsh while at the same time honoring her wishes. Let me talk to her. I think she'll come around. We both know that the flowers aren't the most important part of a reception. It's all about the food. I can't thank you enough for all your assistance. Now ladies, I'd like to invite you to join me in the solarium. I made a buttermilk pie earlier this morning. I don't want to send you away hungry."

Martha Dexter hurried to lead them into the solarium. "I'd like an extra large piece. I'm famished."

Mary Alice and Almeda exchanged knowing looks.

After Almeda had served each of them, Mary Alice asked, "What is this flavor? You've done something different with this pie."

Almeda smiled, " I know that you both will remember that *Southern Buttermilk Pie* was actually a product of The Great Depression. Our mothers and grandmothers had to use the ingredients that were readily available to them. The only additional flavor they could add to the eggs, flour, sugar, and buttermilk might be a little vanilla or nutmeg if they had any. I've added both the vanilla and nutmeg plus just a little something extra that they most likely did not have available."

"Like what?" Martha Dexter asked as she shoved her empty plate across the table to Almeda. "May I have another piece?"

Almeda cut her another slice. "I added a tasteful helping

of *Amaretto* liqueur. As you can see, I've topped my pie with whipped cream and fresh strawberry slices. I added a little *Amaretto* to the whipped cream as well."

"My compliments." Mary Alice nodded.

"Did you use store bought crust?" Martha asked.

"Martha Dexter, when did you know me to ever use anything store bought? No decent Southern cook would ever consider such a thing. No, thank you, I made my crust from scratch."

"Well, it's absolutely delicious. I sure wish I could take my Howard some of this pie."

Almeda shook her head and with a smirk shoved the rest of the pie across the table toward her. "Here. You take the rest of it home with you."

Mary Alice whispered in Almeda's ear, "Some people just suck the nice right out of you."

The Magnolia Series

Dennis R. Maynard

29

Father Steele Austin's Wednesday routine had not varied since his arrival at First Church. His day started at the chapel altar. There he celebrated the seven a.m. Holy Eucharist for a faithful group averaging thirty-five people. This small community within the larger First Church family considered the early Wednesday service to be their Sunday obligation. Some came because their professional choices required them to work on Sundays. Others chose the Wednesday service so that they could enjoy their weekend homes in the Georgia mountains, the Georgia or South Carolina shore, the golf course, or simply because they wanted to avoid the Sunday crowds. There were a few that chose this service because the *1928 Book of Common Prayer* was still being utilized for the Mass.

Following the brief service, the worshippers routinely gathered at *Harry's Cafe*. It was a greasy spoon restaurant that specialized in home cooking. The most popular item on the breakfast menu was the pork sausage biscuit. The biscuits were freshly baked. They were large and flaky. Most chose to order pork sausage biscuits with raspberry jam. Harry always reserved a long table in the dining room for the First Church crowd that usually numbered more than twenty. Conversation at the table always centered on First Church. It gave Steele a wonderful opportunity to quell rumors and to remind those present not to accept gossip as gospel.

Back at his office Steele devoted the rest of the day to the appointments that Crystal had scheduled for him. Appointments began at nine o'clock sharp. Crystal brought two elderly men into his office. She introduced them as Frank Osborn and Steve Livingston. "Please, Gentlemen, sit down. I remember seeing both of you at the eleven o'clock Mass. I've greeted you at the door, but I don't think we've ever had the opportunity to visit at length."

Steve spoke first. "You have a remarkable memory. We didn't think you would remember us at all." Steele studied the two men. They were dressed in suits and ties with well-polished shoes. They could have easily passed as successful businessmen of means. Even at their advanced age, they would be considered strikingly handsome.

"Unless you have some pressing issue let's just spend some time getting to know each other."

The two men glanced at each other. Frank spoke first, "That sounds great. We do have something specific we want to discuss with you. Helping you to know more about us is probably the best place to begin."

"Great. Tell me about yourselves."

"Father Austin, the first thing you need to know is that we are gay. We are a couple. We've been together for over forty years."

"Congratulations. Not many couples this day and time make it that many years. What's your secret?"

Steve chuckled. "Oh, there's no secret. We just made the commitment that any time we had a disagreement we'd talk it out until it was resolved to our mutual satisfaction."

"Obviously that's worked for you. Tell me, how did you meet?"

"We're Marines. We were stationed together in Japan." Steve took Frank's hand as he revealed their story. "I saw this handsome guy in the commissary. It was love at first sight. I asked him to join me for a drink and dinner. We've been together since."

"If you don't mind my asking, how did you survive? I don't mean to offend, but you became a couple at a time when gay men were being threatened, ostracized, beaten, and even murdered."

Steve nodded, "You're right. We had to be careful. Father Austin, over these many years we never apologized for who we are. But we never rubbed our relationship in anyone's face either."

"I understand. I should probably know this, but how long have you been at First Church?"

Steve answered, "I grew up here. I was baptized here at First Church. Back in the day, I was an acolyte and before enlisting in the marines, I sang in the choir. This is my home. My parents were active here as well. They're long since gone. Their remains are buried in the churchyard. When we were both discharged, I asked Frank if he would move to my home in Falls City with me."

"Do any of the members of the church know about your relationship? I have to confess I thought that the two of you were brothers."

Steve and Frank laughed. "A handful of people here in the congregation know about us. Most of them are also gay."

"I hope that we've made you feel welcome and included in this church family."

"Father Austin, you've done more than any other priest we've had here to make us feel welcome."

Steele was confused. "How? I don't know what I could have done any different than any other priest."

"You've preached the entire gospel. You've sought to build a church that welcomes every person that wants to be a member of this community."

"Well, thank you."

They exchanged hesitating looks. Frank asked, "Father Austin, are you familiar with *Integrity*? It's an organization in the national Episcopal Church."

"I am. They want to help insure that our church will be a welcoming place to all people regardless of their sexuality."

"We'd like your permission to establish a chapter here at First Church."

"Why do you feel we need a chapter?"

"Please understand, we're not talking about some sort of activist movement with rainbow flags, floats, and parades. We're thinking about something more low key."

Steve joined the conversation. "We've attended the supper clubs you've organized in the parish. We've actually gone to every one of them. The people were all very nice to us. We just don't belong."

Frank spoke," Don't get us wrong. We love a potluck dinner as much as anyone. It's just that all the folks that attend are married heterosexual couples. We even went to the one that was for singles. But ninety percent of the people there were women looking for a husband. We'd like to have potlucks and activities with people that are more like us."

"How many gay couples do you think there are here at First Church?"

"There are at least seven couples interested in having a chapter of *Integrity* here."

"Seven?"

"Are you surprised?"

"I guess I am. I would have thought two or three others, but certainly not seven."

"Father Austin, if you allow us to do this we think you'll be even more surprised by the number that come forward. Once it's known in the larger community that First Church is a welcoming place that affirms *LGBT* people, we believe more will want to make this parish their church home. As you well know, gay and lesbian people are not welcome in all churches. The Episcopal Church has made it known that you welcome people like us to share in the full life of the Christian Faith."

Steele sat silent. He had no reason not to grant their request, but he knew it wouldn't be without controversy. He could already hear Colonel Mitchell yelling in his ear. "I want to help you organize a chapter of *Integrity* here. But first, I'd like to take the idea to my vestry."

Steve responded, "Father Austin, you're the rector. You don't have to have the vestry's permission to do this."

"You're right. I don't. What you don't know is that there is a lot of turmoil in the parish right now. It's coming primarily from a group in our congregation that's loud and homophobic. They've already confronted the vestry with their demands at our last meeting. I just don't want to do an end run around the vestry. I really need to include them in this decision."

"What do you think they'll say?"

"They're unpredictable. There have been things I thought they would rule one way and they voted to go the other. I hope you understand why I need to do this."

"Do we have your support?"

"You can rest assured that you have my support. I will do all in my power to help you get a chapter of *Integrity* at First Church. I just need you to be patient."

"Father Austin, we've been waiting over sixty years for this parish to openly include us in Her life. We can wait a few more weeks."

The Magnolia Series

Dennis R. Maynard

30

Thackston Willoughby needed some answers. He was in love with his wife, but he was now convinced that she was lying to him. His conversation with Bernice only brought more questions. He knew his wife was hiding something. He didn't know what. Why had she even invited Steele Austin to their home while he was out of the city? Did he really have a heart attack? Since that event, she'd been the perfect wife. That only made him more suspicious. He wanted to talk to the one man that would have the answer.

Thackston was shown into the office of Chief Sparks by one of the desk sergeants. The Chief nodded for him to take a seat opposite his desk. The Chief wasn't completely surprised by the visit. He knew the answer to his first question even before Thackston asked it. "Mister Willoughby, what can I do for you?"

Thackston didn't want to lay all of his cards on the table immediately. He wanted to try to find out as much as he could. "Do you know why Father Austin collapsed at our home?"

"We are still looking into the matter."

"What does that mean?"

"Just as I said. We are still looking into it."

"Did the doctors diagnose his problem?"

"Mister Willoughby, you're an attorney. You know I can't answer that."

"Okay, let me ask the same question in another way. Does Father Austin know what happened to him?"

"Again, I can't answer that."

"If I were to ask Father Austin could he tell me?"

"Tell you what?"

"If he has a medical condition."

"You'd need to ask him directly. Again, I'm not free to discuss his medical condition or any aspect of this case."

"So there is a case?"

The Chief studied Thackston. He chewed slowly on his unlit cigar. Clearly the man sitting before him suspected that something more than a heart attack had occurred. He was also a husband in search of answers. He was a respected attorney with an admirable record. The Chief knew he had to choose his words carefully. "Let me ask if you're acting as your wife's attorney?"

"Does she need an attorney?"

"That wasn't my question. Are you her attorney?"

"Doctors don't operate on family members. An attorney probably shouldn't represent his wife. I admit I have in the past and if required to do so I'll probably do it again. So let me repeat my question again. Does she need one?"

"Mister Willoughby, I can only advise that we are still investigating what happened to Father Austin."

Thackston sat back in his chair. The various pieces to the puzzle were beginning to fall into place in his mind. As Virginia's husband, he was beginning to feel nauseous. As an attorney, he wanted to find out all he could. "So you do have an open investigation?"

Chief Sparks was beginning to have some pity for the husband sitting before him. As the Chief of Police of Falls City, he knew it was essential that he protect his investigation. "Mister Willoughby, we have an open investigation. I'm quite sure you understand just why I can't discuss the details of the case with you."

"Is my wife a suspect in your investigation?"

Chief Sparks was just a bit surprised by his question. Clearly Thackston had been conducting an investigation of his own. Once again he needed to be truthful with him, but policy prohibited him from revealing anything about the investigation. "Mister Willoughby, I can tell you that your wife is a person of interest in our investigation."

"When do you think you'll conclude your inquiry?"

Once again, Chief Sparks was torn between his duties as a law enforcement officer and his pity for the man sitting before him. He decided in favor of pity. "We are waiting on certain lab tests to be returned. Once we have those tests in hand, we'll meet with the District Attorney and turn our findings over to him."

Thackston felt his mouth go dry. "Are you able to advise me as to the type of test results you're waiting on?"

The Chief's heart really went out to him. He was realizing that his wife was not only a person of interest, but she was the center of the investigation. The Chief didn't know what Thackston already knew, but he was certain that he'd gathered enough evidence to make him suspicious of his own wife. The Chief once again went beyond the bounds of what he should have done. "We're waiting on DNA results. We've already received drug related results."

The blood drained from Thackston's face. He'd heard enough to confirm his suspicions. "Chief, when the time does come, will you please call my office? I'll be acting as my wife's attorney." Thackston left Chief Sparks' office. He hurried down the hallway and ran into the nearest men's room. He lost his breakfast in the first available toilet.

The Magnolia Series

Dennis R. Maynard

31

"Honey, did you try on your old *Morning Coat*?" Elmer and Rose were sharing a glass of wine at Rose's home. Doctor Drummond had given them homework to do after their last premarital counseling session.

Elmer chuckled, "I didn't need to. I realized as soon as I took it out of the garment bag it was too big for me. I bought a new one. In fact, I replaced all my formal wear."

"Do you think you're going to need them?"

"Honey, if Almeda has her way we'll be invited to every formal event in Falls City from now on."

"Gosh, I just don't know how comfortable I'm going to be with all that."

"Rose you're a beautiful and gracious lady. Not only will you fit right in but you'll be bringing star power."

"Oh, I don't know about that."

"Well, I do."

"Honey, do you think Father Austin is upset that we asked Doctor Drummond to do our wedding?"

"I don't think he's that kind of guy. Besides, I'm not sure he's all that big on me just yet. The last time I tried to talk to him it was like his mind was someplace else. I know he was listening to me, but there was just something not right."

"Remember, he did have that medical event."

"I do. But to answer your question, I really don't think it'll be a problem for him. You all did live with Doctor and Mrs. Drummond for some time and they've done a lot for you. I think he'll understand. I know Almeda will insist that Randi and Steele come to our reception. I think he'll be fine with it."

"Are you ready to do our homework?"

"Okay, here is the first question. 'Is there any aspect of your current life you'd like to retain in your marriage?' "

Rose sighed. "I've thought a lot about this and I hope it

won't be a problem for you."

"Go on. I can't imagine there's anything about you or your life right now I'd want to change."

"Elmer, I want to keep my clothing business. I want to keep working. My little business started with just me. Now I have three employees. I love what I'm doing and I want to be able to..."

Elmer hugged her. "Of course, I want you to be happy. I want to assure you that I have enough money to take care of you and the children. You don't have to work."

Rose smiled. "I'm not looking for a meal ticket. I just want to marry you. I also want to be able to contribute to our household. You may not need my contribution, but I don't think it's fair that you have to pay for everything. I want to help. It's a matter of pride."

"I have absolutely no problem with your work. I love you. If running your business makes you happy, I'm all for it."

"Thank you. I love you too. Now, what do you want?"

"I've really enjoyed working with John Calvin. I've seen him make a lot of progress with his studies. I'm beginning to think I might have a gift that allows me to work with children with learning disabilities."

"So what are you saying?"

"I sold my business after Judith left me. I don't want another. I don't really need another. I would like to get the necessary education, training, and licensing to be a tutor to children with special needs. I don't expect it would pay very much money, but it's not about the money. It's devoting the rest of my life to helping kids like John Calvin."

Rose put her arms around Elmer's neck and hugged him. "And Mister Idle, you have just given me yet one more reason to love you."

"So it's okay with you?"

"I approve one hundred percent."

Elmer was quiet. He stared off in space. Rose took his hand. "Elmer, Honey, what is it?"

"There is one more thing I want us to talk about. It's not

a part of the assignment Doctor Drummond gave us. But Rose, it's been on my mind a lot. I have a question I really want to ask you, but I'm hesitant."

"Go on."

Elmer looked into her eyes. "Rose, you know that I love your children."

"I know. I like it when you call them 'our children'."

"Rose, remember I told you that when I was married to Judith I wanted children, but she didn't."

"I remember."

"It's left a dark hole in my life. I'd like to have children to carry on my family name. I want children to call me *Daddy*."

"I understand."

"Rose, are you going to change your last name after we're married?"

"I've played with it in my mind, Rose Idle. It sounds strange. But then my children will still go by their father's name. I have no affection for the MacClaren name, but I'm not sure I want my children to have a different last name than me. I think that could cause them problems with their friends."

"What if we could fix that?"

"How?"

"Do you think I could legally adopt your children as my own? I promise you that I will always love and cherish them as if they are my own flesh."

"I know you would. We'll have to see if Melvin will allow it. There's a part of me that thinks he just might. He didn't even ask to see the children when he was here in Falls City. I know they didn't want to see him. I believe they already think of you as their father. John Calvin asked me again if he could call you *Daddy* after we get married."

A tear rolled down Elmer's face. "I can't tell you how much that would mean to me. Is it okay with you if I ask my attorney to investigate the possibility?"

"Of course it is. We can change all their names to your last name. I'll take your last name. We'll be one family with the same last name."

"I love you so much." Elmer's mouth began to quiver. "I want us to be a family."

Rose smiled and squeezed his hand. "And the best part is that our three children will have the same last name as their little brother or sister."

Elmer nodded. "Yes, that would really be nice." Elmer lay quietly smiling and thinking about his new family. He was feeling happy and content. Suddenly he was jolted from his thoughts with a jerk. His eyes widened. He stared at Rose. Then he jumped to his feet. He shouted, "Wait! What did you say?"

The Magnolia Series

Dennis R. Maynard

32

"I promised that I would get back to you after I met with the rector." Colonel Mitchell had called another meeting of those unhappy with The Episcopal Church. Only about one hundred people were in attendance at this meeting.

"As I predicted, the rector was completely unwilling to decrease the giving to the diocese. He would not even let the vestry consider cutting our giving to the National Church."

"I don't want any of the money I put in the offering plate going to either one of them," a man shouted. Many nods and even a few *Amens* followed that comment.

Colonel Mitchell was pleased with the response he was getting. "I think it would be a positive exercise for us to simply make a list of the changes at First Church and The Episcopal Church that cause us concern. I'm going to record them on this newsprint."

"I'd like to begin," a man responded. "I opposed that soup kitchen and I still do. I have reason to believe that it's one of the reasons the number of homeless in this city has increased. They're standing on virtually every corner in this city begging for money. It's so irritating."

Another man chided, "We had better not forget that AIDS service he had for all the homosexuals. We didn't have any of their kind coming to First Church until he did that."

"Well, I opposed that free medical clinic. My husband is a doctor. He's constantly criticized because he won't volunteer to work in it. It's not fair. He's busy enough."

"What about those Habitat Houses he's always trying to get built?" An elderly man could not hide his disgust. "I had to work my entire life to pay for a home. Now he's just out there giving houses away to people who are too lazy to work." The man continued, "Don't forget that hotel he opened up for gay kids. Whoever heard of a church providing teenagers a place to hold their sinful orgies?"

Colonel Mitchell was pleased with the developing list. "These are all issues that have upset many of us. Now let's focus on the changes that Austin has brought to First Church. Let's list some of those."

"I told you all at the last meeting that I refuse to take communion from a female priestess. It's not right. I don't think it's a matter of whether or not women should be priests. I think we need to accept the fact that they cannot be priests. It's not possible for a woman to be a priest. You can't baptize a person with *Co-cola.* You cannot have a valid Eucharist with grape juice instead of wine. And female flesh cannot be ordained to the priesthood! Read your Bible!"

Another man stood and grew red in the face. "I'm not ashamed to say it, but I will. I don't think it was right that he buried those Negroes in our sacred cemetery. That cemetery is hallowed ground. Only members of First Church and their descendants should be buried in our churchyard."

"Don't forget the rumor that he also buried a cat in our cemetery," a woman seethed.

"Did you all enjoy showing up a few years back for the Christmas Eve Mass only to discover that all the seats were taken up by a bunch of blacks? Do you all remember when he invited their choir to sing at the Midnight Mass in our church?"

The elderly man that had objected to the Habitat Houses stood. His hands were visibly shaking. "This is all well and good. What are we going to do about it?"

The room erupted with murmurs of agreement. Colonel Mitchell held up his hand. "I'm sending around copies of a sheet that I received just before this meeting from one of the office volunteers. This pamphlet was mailed out this afternoon to the vestry. It's in their packet for the upcoming meeting. It's information on *Integrity.* They're a group for homosexuals in the Episcopal Church."

"What is this, Colonel?" A man shouted with disgust.

"As I said, it's going out to the vestry. Steele Austin is advising them that he's starting a club for homosexuals at First

Church."

"Enough!" A man stood and tore the sheet into multiple pieces. "Colonel, I can take no more. What are we going to do? My family has no choice but to join another church."

The room exploded with others expressing their anger. Colonel Mitchell once again motioned for quiet. "I think I have an answer that will make us all happy. My friends, I'd like to introduce a guest. Please welcome The Venerable Peter John Fox. He is currently the rector of Saint Augustine's Anglican Church in Atlanta."

Following a polite round of applause, a thirty-something man stood next to Colonel Mitchell. He was wearing a black suit and black clerical shirt. His collar had a hint of purple lining under it. "Mister Mitchell, thank you for inviting me to this meeting. My fellow Christians, I am a priest in the Missionary Anglican Church. We have four churches in the State of Georgia. We are a Church that proclaims that the Old and New Testaments are the inspired Word of God. The teachings of scripture are not to be subjected to liberal bias. The Holy Word of God is a sufficient foundation for our faith. We have an all-male priesthood. It's preposterous to think that a woman can be a priest. She can dress up like a priest, but that does not make her one. I can dress up like a cowboy, but that doesn't make me one. We believe life is sacred. Life begins at conception. Please understand that the Missionary Anglican Church is not trying to control a woman's body or women's health care. We believe that the life in a mother's womb is a baby. He or she is a human being with a soul. Our primary concern is protecting the life of the unborn baby. That baby is not a part of her body. It is a separate soul temporarily residing in her womb. For that reason alone we reject the politically correct term *Fetus*. Finally, we also teach that gay and lesbian behavior is contrary to God's will. That will never be up for debate in the Missionary Anglican Church."

The room exploded with applause. Father Peter John Fox smiled. "I believe that our time will be most profitable if I simply answer your questions. So please, let's begin."

Hands went up all over the room. He pointed to the first person. "Are you a part of The Episcopal Church?"

"No. We do use the Book of Common Prayer and wear the same vestments as Episcopal clergy. Our governance is the same, but we're not Episcopalians. We are Anglicans."

"So are you a part of Anglican Communion?"

"No. The Archbishop of Canterbury does not recognize us as part of the larger communion. We decided that being faithful to the teachings of Jesus is more important than being faithful to some archbishop."

"Then how can you call yourself Anglican?"

"Our priests and bishops are in apostolic succession. Most of our clergy are former Episcopal priests who can no longer tolerate the heresies being promulgated in that church. Our sponsoring bishops are in The Anglican Church in Africa. Our newly ordained priests and bishops can trace the historic episcopate through them."

"So they're part of the Anglican Communion?"

"Yes. But they're so concerned about the direction of The Episcopal Church here in America they have designated us as a mission field. Their objective is to establish churches here in the United States that will adhere to the teachings of Jesus and not the various whims of society. Don't you think it ironic that we used to send missionaries to Africa to try to save the people there? Now they're sending missionary bishops to us to help save the Church in America."

"Colonel, you must have a plan. What is it?"

Colonel Mitchell looked out across the room. He could see that all present were anxious to hear his plan. At last he'd get even with that phony rector at First Church. He would also insure himself a position of distinction in the history of the Christian Church in Falls City.

The Magnolia Series

Dennis R. Maynard

CHAPTER

33

Virginia Willoughby was horny. She needed a man. She wanted to feel a man want her. Her husband had not made her feel that way for days. Since he'd subjected her to that cross-examination about Father Austin, he'd changed. He did not look at her in the same way. He stopped telling her that he loved her. Even the hugs and pecks on the cheek he gave her were quick and lacked feeling.

But he'd changed in other ways as well. She felt like he was always watching her. She even felt like he was listening in on her telephone calls. She tried to tell herself she was just being paranoid, but her intuition told her otherwise. She was sure that he was trying to catch her doing something wrong. She'd tried to be the perfect wife since the event with the priest. She'd tried to dress more seductively in the bedroom. But even when she came out of her dressing closet completely naked and stood before him, he only glanced up from the book he was reading and then went right back to it.

Virginia wanted to hear a man tell her she's beautiful. She wanted to feel a man's eyes run over her body and lust for it. She desperately needed to feel a man's desire plunging into her. If Thackston was not going to satisfy her she'd find someone that would. Her husband had to fly up to Richmond for the day. Virginia knew exactly what she needed to do to take advantage of his absence.

Sitting right at the first of the four exits off the freeway to Falls City is a huge truck stop. In addition to all the fueling and repair services a trucker might need, there is a cafe with a bar, and a motel. Virginia knew that most any time of the day it would be filled with at least a dozen burly truckers. They would be lonely and open to female companionship.

Virginia dressed in one of her most seductive outfits for her trip to the truck stop bar. She chose one of her tightest sweaters. She did not wear a bra under it. She chose a red sweater. She'd read in a magazine for women that the color red stimulates sexual desire. She knew that her legs and her breasts were her most desirous qualities. She wore shorts that just barely covered her behind. In fact, when she turned to look in her full-length mirror, she could see that some of her butt cheek was visible. Her four-inch heels accented her legs.

As soon as Virginia walked through the swinging doors separating the bar from the cafe, she felt every man's eyes on her. One of the truckers gave her a low whistle. She smiled at him appreciatively. Virginia positioned herself on the end barstool so that her body would be visible to all in the bar. She crossed her legs and leaned forward so that her breasts thrust forward. She ordered a glass of soda water with a lime. She wanted to be completely sober for her seduction.

Virginia turned on the barstool so that she could choose her target. She was immediately attracted to a man at the end of the bar. He had curly black hair, blue eyes, and bulging biceps. Virginia made eye contact with him and stared deep into his eyes. She smiled seductively at him. He immediately moved to the seat next to her. "Tell me, Pretty Lady, what are you doing in a place like this?"

"Can't a girl get a drink when she's thirsty?"

He pointed at the glass sitting on the bar in front of her, "I don't think that qualifies as a drink. So I'll ask you one more time, why are you here?"

Virginia leaned toward him. She knew her breasts were straining against her tight sweater. She saw his eyes drop down to them. She whispered seductively in his ear, "Maybe I'm just looking for a good time."

"Are you a working girl?"

Virginia giggled. "Absolutely not."

"So you're a vice cop."

That brought forth a full-throated laugh. "Do I look like a cop? Lock up your paranoia, Cowboy. I'm not a cop."

"Okay, so who do you want to get even with? Did your husband cheat on you or was it your boyfriend?"

"Neither." She ran her fingers over his cheek. "I'm just a girl looking for a nice afternoon."

"And I'm positive that a woman like you either has a boyfriend or husband. So which one is out of town today?"

"Well, aren't you smart? Does it really matter to you?"

"No, I guess it doesn't."

Virginia placed her hand on his leg. She slowly moved her hand up his leg to his crotch. "My, oh my, have you started without me?"

The man smiled, "That happened when you walked into this bar. It's your fault. Just looking at you did it to me."

Virginia let out a low squeal and snickered. That was just what she'd needed to hear a man say. She whispered seductively, "So do you think you're man enough to satisfy a woman like me?"

"What did you have in mind?"

"Let's get a room and see what happens."

"My truck is being fueled right now. I need to move it out of the bay. You get a room. Register at the front desk as *Mrs. Smith*. I'll join you as soon as I move my truck."

"*Mrs. Smith*?" Virginia smirked, "Aren't you a creative genius? My guess is you've done this before. Okay, I'll register as *Mrs. Smith*, but you need to hurry."

Virginia registered at the motel desk. The clerk asked for her identification. She told him she doesn't have one. She doesn't know how to drive a car, but her husband would be joining her. The clerk could ask for his driver's license. She told him she didn't have a credit card either, but she could pay cash. The clerk grabbed her money and put it in his pocket. He handed her a key.

In the room she couldn't decide whether she should get undressed or let the trucker undress her. She decided on the latter. As soon as the man entered the room he immediately pulled her sweater off her. His face went directly to her breasts. She gently lifted his face so she could open his shirt. He pushed her back on the bed and pulled her shorts down. In seconds he was in her, thrusting. Almost as quickly she heard him moan and then he pulled away. "Is that all?" Virginia complained.

The man was quickly pulling his jeans back up. He'd not even bothered to completely remove them. He buckled his belt, "That's all I need."

Virginia couldn't believe her eyes and ears. She'd come for romance and he'd simply used her as a sperm disposal. "Is that the way you treat your wife?"

"Leave my wife out of this."

"So is it?"

"I love my wife. What she doesn't know doesn't hurt her. As far as I'm concerned you're just a freebie. You're nothing but a whore that's too stupid to charge."

"Wait! You need to reimburse me for this room. I paid cash. You owe me eighty dollars."

"Lady, I'm not going to reimburse you. I'm not paying for anything. God, just how stupid are you? Any professional knows to get her *John* to pay for the room up front. What kind of cheap trick are you? It wouldn't surprise me to learn that you invite your boyfriends into the same bed you share with your husband. Woman, even the worst trailer park slut doesn't lower herself to that level."

"You can't talk to me that way."

"I can do anything I want with you or to you. You've already made that perfectly clear."

"You need to reimburse me for this room. Give me my money."

The trucker snorted, "You really are a piece of work. I feel sorry for your husband." He opened the door, "You've got the room for the next twenty-four hours. Maybe you can go back down to the bar and find some poor sucker that'll pay for it. Frankly, I don't think you're worth it. In fact, right now you disgust me." He didn't bother to look back or close the door.

Virginia caught her reflection in the mirror opposite the bed. She broke down sobbing.

The Magnolia Series

Dennis R. Maynard

34

Stone Clemons seldom made an appointment to see Steele Austin. He preferred to call the rector's secretary to determine when he was going to be free. Then he simply showed up at the door. Stone was one of Steele's strongest supporters. In addition to being an expert on the Episcopal Church's ecclesiastical laws, few things happened in Falls City without his knowledge. Steele looked up from his desk and saw Stone walking into his office. He rose to greet him. "Let's sit over here." Steele pointed to the wingback chairs in his office. "We'll be more comfortable. Do you want something to drink?"

Stone grinned. "No, *Faaather*, I don't need anything, but thanks for asking." Stone enjoyed stretching the word Father. "*Faaather*, have you heard about the insurance agent that decided to make a sales call on a real cowboy on a working ranch?"

"No, I don't think I have."

"Well, after the cowboy filled in the application the agent reviewed it. 'I notice you've written that you've never had an accident.'

'Yep. No accidents.'

'I have to tell you that I find it hard to believe that on this working ranch you've never been injured.'

The cowboy's eyes lit up. 'Oh, a rattlesnake bit me one time. And on another I was kicked by a horse.'

'You don't call those accidents?'

'Heck no, they both did it on purpose.' "

Steele laughed and nodded. "That's a good one. I may have to use it in my sermon."

"It's all yours."

"Okay, I don't think you came over here just to share a story. What do you know that I don't know?"

"Well *suh*, I do have some information. You're going to have to decide if it's good news or bad news. It appears to me you're about to have a great big pus-filled blister removed from your butt."

Steele chuckled, "Now you have my interest."

"It seems that the president of your fan club is taking a few dozen or your members and starting a new church."

"Who? What?"

"You heard me correctly. Your old nemesis has been meeting with quite a number of folks who are unhappy with The Episcopal Church, the diocese, and you. Since you and the vestry refuse to yield to their desires, Colonel Mitchell is showing them how start their own church."

"What kind of church?"

"They're joining up with one of those dissident groups out of Africa. They have one of their Anglican bishops as their *pope*."

"How many people are we talking about?"

"I don't know for sure, but it could be close to a hundred or more."

"How do you know this? I haven't heard anything about it."

"One of the real estate attorneys in my office advised me. They've made an offer on that Lutheran Church they shut down over off First Avenue last year."

"Wow! This is big."

"Like I said, you're going to have to decide whether it's good news or bad news."

"I have to confess never having to deal with Colonel Mitchell again is a pleasant thought."

"I couldn't agree more."

"You know that every healthy system has a method for getting rid of infections."

"How do you think the rest of the congregation is going to respond to this news?"

"We're going to find out soon."

"How's that?"

"One of my paralegals is married to a reporter over at the newspaper. They're running a story this Saturday on the new church."

"Are you connected to every person and organization in this town?"

Stone smiled knowingly. "I like to stay informed."

"I can read the story now. This new church is the result of the liberal movement in the Episcopal Church. They're going to bash all the things that most of us consider to be positive and good."

"Well, you're going to get your chance. I've asked that same reporter to do a story on you and The Episcopal Church the following Saturday."

"Thanks. I'll look forward to it. My immediate concern is talking with the congregation about all this. I know they're going to come to church Sunday morning wanting to hear my thoughts. I've got to get them together. I also need to call the bishop and bring him into the loop."

"I know you'll come up with the right words. It's going to be hard for some of our members since they're friends with a few of those that will be leaving. Others are going to be angry. And of course, there will be those that blame you."

Steele nodded sadly. "I know. The buck stops here."

Stone and Steele sat in silence for a few minutes. Stone cleared his throat. "There's one more thing I need to discuss with you."

"Okay."

"I spoke with the Chief before I came over. He has all the tests back. He's reviewed his investigation with the District Attorney. They'd like to set up a meeting with Randi and you at your earliest convenience."

"Will you be there?"

"I'm your attorney. I'll be there."

"What do they want from me?"

"They're going to ask if you're willing to testify against Virginia Willoughby."

Steele wrinkled his brow. "What are you saying? I don't

understand. I can only tell what I know happened. Why would I testify against her?"

"Once you've heard the results of all the tests and go over their investigative notes, you'll understand."

"Understand what?"

"Father, that woman drugged you and then tried to rape you."

The Magnolia Series

Dennis R. Maynard

CHAPTER

35

"Randi, Honey, where are the children?"

"Travis is still in preschool. Amanda is on a play date with one of her friends. I'll need to pick them up in a couple of hours."

"So you're free to come down to my office?"

"I guess so. Do I need to? What's going on?"

"Stone is here right now. The Chief and a prosecutor from the District Attorney's office are coming here to my office. They've concluded their investigation about what happened to me. They want to go over their results with us."

"Do you know what happened to you?"

"I do now."

"Tell me."

"Randi, I'd better not do that over the phone. You need to hear it from them."

"Okay, I'll be there in about twenty minutes."

"Take your time. Chief Sparks and the prosecutor from the District Attorney's office aren't here yet."

Randi walked into Steele's office. Stone, the Chief, and the prosecutor all stood. Randi hugged the Chief and Stone and kissed Steele on the cheek. The prosecutor introduced herself. "Mrs. Austin, I'm Laura Atkins from the prosecutor's office."

Stone suggested that they all sit over at the conference table. "We'll need the table surface to examine the results of our investigation."

Randi was impatient. "If you all know what happened to my husband, I want to know that first. Tell me what happened to him."

"Wouldn't you rather go through the notes from our investigation and examine the test results first?" Stone asked.

"No, I want the bottom line. What happened to him?"

Steele took Randi's hand. "Honey, they've discovered that Virginia drugged me and then tried to rape me."

Large tears ran down Randi's cheeks. "Oh Steele, no."

All sat silent while Randi wept. Steele put his arm around her and held her close to him. She leaned on his shoulder as the tears flowed. Tears welled up in Steele's eyes as well. When Randi composed herself, she wiped her eyes and asked, "I just want to know if she was successful."

The Chief answered, "No Randi, we don't believe she was."

"You don't believe? What does that mean?"

"Please, let's go through the investigation and you'll see why we don't have any evidence she was able to complete the task."

Randi nodded, "Okay, but I need to know one thing first. How long was she alone with my unconscious husband?"

Stone answered, "We know that GHB, that's what the tests show she gave Steele, can become active in as little as ten minutes. It can take longer depending on the amount used and the weight of the victim. We also know she put it in the glass of tea that she gave him to drink. The examination at the hospital concluded that he had an empty stomach. The drug knocked him out in minutes."

"What? That doesn't answer my question."

The Chief responded, "We know Steele was supposed to arrive at the Willoughby home at 11:30 a.m. We also know that Steele left his office at 11:15 a.m., so he arrived on time. The 911 call was placed by Mister Willoughby from his home at 12:05 p.m. If we allow ten minutes or so for the drug to kick in, we're talking about 11:40 to 11:45 before the drug took effect. That means she only had twenty minutes at most to be alone with him."

"How far did she get?"

The Chief wrinkled his brow. "What are you asking?"

"I want to know just how far she got with my husband while he was lying there unconscious."

Stone wanted to reassure her. He leaned toward her. In

a calming voice he answered her question, "None of her DNA was found below his waist."

"But her DNA was found on his chest?"

Stone nodded.

"His neck?"

Stone nodded again.

"My husband's lips?"

Stone nodded yet again.

Randi gritted her teeth as she spoke to the prosecutor. "Miss Atkins, I want you to put that bitch behind bars for the rest of her life! Just who does she think she is? What kind of woman does this sort of thing? What kind of woman even wants to have sex with another woman's husband? That woman tried to take advantage of my husband while he was unconscious. I want you to teach her a lesson she won't soon forget."

The prosecutor nodded knowingly. "This sort of thing is a lot more common than most people realize. Obviously, most rapes are committed by males against females. The second is males against males. But female rape of males is well documented. They usually use drugs or alcohol to incapacitate their victim. It's more common for an older woman to rape a younger man, but it also happens when a suitor has rebuffed them. We have reason to believe that this is the case here. Your husband did not respond to her the way she wanted so she decided to take matters into her own hands."

Stone cleared his throat. "Randi, we have to think this through. If you and Steele want the prosecutor to take this to trial, that's exactly what we'll do. But we've got to consider the unintended consequences. It will become front-page news. I can see the headlines now, *Church Member Attempts To Rape Parish Priest*. Your photo and Steele's photo will be on the cover of every magazine. They'll be staring back at you every time you go to the grocery store."

"I don't care. I want her to pay for this. She needs to be behind bars."

Steele squeezed Randi's hand, "Honey, I feel the same

way, but we also have to think about Travis and Amanda. If this story becomes the headline that the people at this table think it will, we won't be able to keep this from them."

The tears flowed down Randi's cheeks. "That's just not fair. Steele, we can't let her get by with this. She has to pay."

"But what about our children?"

Randi wiped the tears from her cheeks, "I would never do anything to hurt them. I know we've got to protect them. I don't want to let her get by with this either."

The prosecutor spoke, "I won't be able to protect them from the press. This will be big news if it gets out. The press will have a field day with it."

More tears rolled down Randi's cheeks, "Then what are we going to do? I want her punished. Steele, don't you want her to go to prison for trying to do this to you?"

Steele nodded, "I most definitely do."

"So that's your decision?" The prosecutor asked. "You want to testify against her?"

Steele stared into Randi's eyes. "Do you agree?"

Randi wiped her eyes. "But Steele, what are we going to do to protect our babies?"

The Magnolia Series

Dennis R. Maynard

CHAPTER

36

"Bishop Powers, thanks so much for calling me back." Bishop Powers was Steele's former bishop in Oklahoma. He had remained a close friend and spiritual advisor. Steele often telephoned him when he needed counsel and direction.

"Steele, you're one of my boys. You can call me at any time. How are Randi and the children?"

"Physically everyone is fine. I really need to talk with you about our emotional health."

"Your marriage is good, right?"

"Oh, our marriage couldn't be better. We're in love with each other. Randi is my soul mate and best friend."

"And how about the antagonists in your parish, are they at it again?"

"I don't think they'll ever stop. They're now demanding we cancel our financial support of the diocese and National Church. They're also wanting us to denounce gays, women clergy, and a couple of other hotbed issues in their attempt to separate this parish from the National Church."

"How's your vestry responding to that?"

"It's a no-go, but it doesn't matter. A bunch of them are leaving and starting their own church. They're uniting with one of those apostate groups sponsored by an African Bishop."

"You may not think of it this way just yet, but that could turn out to be one of the best gifts you've received."

"I have to confess there are a couple of those folks I will not miss. When I was ordained it never occurred to me that as a priest I would make enemies. Bishop, I'm convinced that some of these people are going to continue to attack me, my ministry, and character even after they change churches."

"Steele, they're not even going to stop after you've done so."

"What do you mean?"

"Just that. Son, they're going to continue to discredit you every time you cross their minds for the rest of their lives."

"For the life of me I don't know what I ever did to offend them."

"Sure you do. Think about it."

"You refused to do their bidding. You didn't tell them what they wanted to hear. And, last but not least, you started ministries for people they find unacceptable."

"I thought I was just trying to be faithful to the teachings of Christ."

Bishop Powers snickered, "And how do you think that worked out for Him?"

"Steele, the same motives that led to the crucifixion of Jesus apply to your antagonists. Perhaps it's just a simple matter of jealousy. Or it could be that you refused to be their lap dog and parrot their understanding of truth. Whatever the reason, any pastor that remains faithful to the ministry and teachings of Jesus is going to make enemies."

"But you'd think that's exactly what a Christian would want to hear and see their priest do."

Steele heard Bishop Powers inhale the smoke from the cigarette he was smoking. "Let me ask you, Father. Do you remember the words Jesus used when he commissioned His disciples for ministry?"

"You're thinking of some specific words."

"I am. He told them that He was sending them out like sheep among wolves. Steele, none of us want to think that there are wolves disguised as sheep in the Church, but I fear there are."

"I would like to think they're just misguided."

"Wouldn't we all, but I've been in ministry long enough to know that evil exists. If I were the devil I'd focus on the ministries of clergy that I perceive to be a threat."

"I think there's a compliment in that statement."

"The answer is yes. Steele, as a bishop, I have clergy in charge of congregations that are quite content to 'tickle the ears' of their listeners. I doubt they will ever make an enemy.

In the eyes of their members they are beloved."

"I guess I'm not cut from that piece of cloth."

"You need only have to reexamine your sermons and your ministry to know you aren't."

"So how is a priest supposed to respond to those that want to destroy them?"

"Steele, Jesus told us to pray for those that persecute us. He didn't command us to house them in our guest room. Likewise, we must not let them take up residence in our mind. I want you to continue to exercise a faithful ministry. Be happy and successful in spite of them. But keep your distance. Don't let them back in your life."

"That sounds like wise counsel."

Once again he could hear Bishop Powers exhale the smoke from his cigarette. "Steele, I met your bishop. There's a lot of speculation about him."

"Oh?"

"Don't worry, I'm not going to ask you about it. Let's just say that there is some conversation."

"Let me tell you that I think he's a really good guy. I think the majority of the clergy in this diocese appreciate his leadership and pastoral care. He's been very supportive of me and for that I'm grateful."

"That's good to hear."

"All through our most recent trauma he's been nothing but helpful."

"Okay. Tell me about that."

"Bishop, it's going to be difficult for me to tell you about this latest chapter. I'm having a tough time believing it myself."

"I'm listening."

"There's this woman in the parish that has somewhat of a whispered reputation. She's married. Most folks speculate that her husband doesn't even know how promiscuous she's been."

"I know the type. They can be dangerous. Male clergy have to be very cautious around them."

"Well, you're getting ahead of me."

"Go on."

"Randi and my secretary both warned me about her. They believe that she's been flirting with me. She even did so right in front of Randi. I promised my wife I would never be alone with her."

"And?"

"I've been trying to raise funds to build another Habitat House here in Falls City. Her husband gave me a check that would cover about half of the project. She called me a couple of weeks ago. She wanted me to come over to their house for lunch. She said they wanted to give me the rest of the money and pay for the entire project."

"That's very generous."

"Yes, it would have been if it were true."

"I asked her if her husband would be there. She said that both her husband and her maid would be there. Her maid would be fixing lunch."

"Was it a set up?"

"It was worse than that. When I arrived, her maid was there and answered the door. The table was all set for three people. Her husband was supposed to be in the library on the telephone. She gave me a glass of iced sweet tea. The next thing I remember is waking up in the emergency room."

"What was in the tea?"

"GHB."

"The date rape drug?"

"Yes."

"They did a full rape kit on me at the hospital. It's taken a few weeks to get all the tests back, but it's conclusive. She tried to rape me."

"That woman is really disturbed."

"I agree. I'd never heard of a woman attempting to rape a man. The rape crisis counselor they sent to talk with Randi and me gave us more information on the subject. It's certainly not as common as male rape of women or even males raping other males, but it's more common than I ever imagined. The counselor gave us some information on a few highly publicized cases of women raping a man. Most of the time they do it while the man is incapacitated with alcohol or drugs."

"So in your case she used a drug?"

"Yes."

"Steele, was she successful?"

"No. Her DNA was left on some pretty embarrassing places, but the evidence is that she did not succeed."

"And you don't remember anything?"

"Absolutely nothing."

"What stopped her?"

"As I understand it, her husband, who was supposed to be out of town, came home early and surprised her."

"How did she explain it?"

"That she thought I was having a heart attack and she was giving me CPR."

"Wow. You've got to give her credit for quick thinking."

"I really think she's a pathological liar. I think she's the type of person that would tell you a lie when the truth would serve her better."

"How has Randi responded to all this?"

"With mixed emotions. At first she was worried about me. Then she got angry with me for not being more careful around the woman. Now she just wants to insure the woman goes to prison."

"So you're going to testify against her?"

"That's what I want to talk with you about. I'd like to see her behind bars."

"But?"

"Bishop, she's ill. I'm not so sure she isn't suffering from multiple personality disorder. Obviously her superego is poorly developed. She probably doesn't allow herself to accept responsibility for any of her behavior. I doubt she has ever felt guilty about anything. I'm just not sure prison is going to do much to change her. On top of it all is the fact that she was sent to prison once before."

"What?"

"She went to prison on a murder for hire scheme. She

was released after it was discovered that she was framed."

"Was she?"

"The judge thought so. I don't know what to think about that incident. I do know for a fact that she cheated on her first husband multiple times."

"She sounds like a real mess."

"What are you going to do?"

"I'm not sure."

"Steele, it's your decision, but from what you've told me she doesn't sound like someone that knows how to control her own impulses. She sounds more like someone who gives in to her every temptation. My hunch is that she does whatever she wants and then lies to herself and anyone who challenges her. From where I'm sitting, that's scary."

"Thanks, Bishop."

"I'll keep you in my prayers. Call me if you need me."

The Magnolia Series

Dennis R. Maynard

CHAPTER

37

"As you can see, I'm not Father Steele Austin." Doctor Horace Drummond was standing in the pulpit of First Church looking out at the gathered congregation. "The worship leaflet says the rector is scheduled to preach this morning. I wrestled the pulpit from him." The congregation chuckled. Steele was sitting in the presiding minister's chair. He smiled broadly and gave Horace a *thumbs up.*

"I know that all of you read the story about the members of our congregation that have left us to start a new church. As you look around this morning you'll see that some familiar faces are missing. I can tell you that many of the folks that are forming the new church are excited about their fresh start. It has been a more painful choice for others. They did not want to leave First Church or The Episcopal Church, but because of their convictions, they believed they had no other choice. Their leaving is painful for many of us. We will miss seeing them in worship and at parish activities."

Horace paused. Then he continued, "I asked the rector if I could preach this morning because I've been a member of the Episcopal Church many more years than he's been alive. I was baptized in this church as an infant. The church I was baptized, confirmed, and ordained in was not the same church that we have today. We need to acknowledge that. Some of you, like me, will remember a different Episcopal Church. When I was ordained we used the *1928 Book of Common Prayer* at worship. Many of you will remember it. We loved that Prayer Book. Some of us were quite convinced that it was the one that Jesus himself used." Several in the congregation chuckled again.

"We all took pride in having our own leather-bound copy of the Prayer Book. Our names were engraved on the cover in gold leaf. We carried it to worship on Sundays and kept it on our bedside table to use during the week. We took pride in being able to memorize the more familiar prayers in the liturgy. There was value in being able to bring forth the most utilized prayers when they were needed. We were quite literally a *People of the Book*. We knew that familiarity bred affection, comfort, and devotion.

Things have changed through the decades. Some of us remember being subjected to *The 1967 Trial Liturgy*, then *The Green Book*, followed by *The Zebra Book*, and then *The Blue Book*. For many of us that was a painful period. Finally, our beloved prayer book was replaced by the *1979 Prayer Book* that we use today. Only we don't use the latest *Prayer Book*. It has multiple options.

On a given Sunday, we don't have a clue as to which part of the *Prayer Book* the priest is going to utilize. The fact is they may not use any of it. They might borrow from another nation's book, some other resource, or make up their own. So little service booklets replaced our beloved Prayer Book. These booklets were soon replaced with service leaflets that had different prayers most every Sunday. In many churches video screens and overhead projectors have replaced these leaflets. Some of us old-timers still long for those days when we were *People of the Book*. Now we are becoming people of the overhead projector. Gone are the leather-bound books with our names engraved on them. Gone but not forgotten are the familiar prayers that we could recite from memory."

Horace could see several nods of agreement from the older members of the congregation. "Some of us remember when women and girls always covered their heads when they entered a House of Worship. Boxes of prayer scarves were kept by the narthex doors for any woman that might have forgotten hers.

Women had a limited ministry in the Episcopal Church. Only men and boys could be acolytes, lay readers, chalice bearers, deacons, priests, and bishops. Women's ministries were restricted to the annual bazaar, Bible study groups, the ECW, and the altar guild. Speaking of the altar guild, back then the only people permitted behind the altar rail were members of the clergy and altar guild members.

Children went to Sunday School during the Mass. Our services were intended to be free of distractions. We prided ourselves on having a quiet church. Everyone could enjoy the service without being distracted by noisy children. Children were brought into the church to find their parents in time for communion. They did not receive communion, but they were given a blessing. The only people that received communion were those that had been confirmed by a bishop."

Horace looked up at the balcony and pointed to it. "For those of you sitting up there in the balcony, you may not know this, but those seats were originally reserved for people like me. You are sitting in what was once known as *The Colored Section.*"

Horace paused again to let the people reflect on his words. "And as for music, the only music allowed in worship was in our authorized hymnal. Now we have praise books, gospel hymns, and the twangs of electronic music often played through the sound system. When we used our old hymnal, the priest could choose from a handful of Mass Settings that were easy for most any voice to sing. Once again, there was comfort in those familiar notes. We could sing most any of them without even opening the hymnal. I know some of you will not understand the following statement, but there are Sundays I still yearn for *Willan, Merbecke*, and a liberal sprinkling of *Shubert.*

It's not unusual today for a different Mass Setting to be chosen each Sunday. Too often the average worshipper will not be able to sing them. They have been written for the trained choir. Only the musically educated can sing along with the choir. Instead of singing those familiar and comforting musical prayers in worship, we often feel like spectators at a concert. It appears to me that the only Mass Setting suitable for congregational singing today is the one written by Robert J. Powell."

Horace leaned over the pulpit. "I remember a time

when everyone stood when a priest or bishop entered the room. That respect was swallowed up in the clergy scandals that had more to do with television evangelists than the priests of our church.

Brothers and sisters, this is the point of the preceding ecclesiastical history lesson. The Church of Jesus Christ is a living organism. As such, the Church evolves and changes in response to new understandings of the Gospel. With new discoveries in science, psychology, and sociology, fresh new insights are brought to the teachings of Christ.

It was just a few decades ago that the *Psychiatric Handbook* listed homosexuality as a mental illness and often treated it as such. Mental Health Professionals taught that dominating mothers and passive fathers turned otherwise normal children into homosexuals. None of us believe that today. New knowledge brings new applications. One of the cornerstones of Anglicanism is that we base our teachings on the three-legged stool of scripture, tradition, and reason.

Our Episcopal Church has evolved and changed. Many of us think for the better. That does not mean we don't cherish our past. In today's Episcopal Church divorced persons are no longer excommunicated. Children attend Mass and receive communion. Women are ordained priests and bishops. And yes, gay and lesbian people are welcomed into the full sacramental life of the church.

This parish, no, your parish has started a soup kitchen, a free medical clinic, and provided housing for the homeless. Along with the larger Episcopal Church, this congregation has stood up against bigotry, racism, and prejudice in any form. These ministries of mercy have not been received well and supported by all. Some of these works and policies for good were initiated in spite of the vigorous protests by some of our most faithful members.

Obviously, there are those that cannot accept one or more of these. They could not accept them then and they cannot accept them now. That is the reason some of our members have chosen to leave and begin a church that more conforms to their beliefs. It is not for us to pass judgment on their decision. In our charity we must wish them well in their new endeavor. If they were our friends yesterday, then as loving Christians, we are called to be their friends today.

Their leaving also provides us with the opportunity to reaffirm the values that undergird our journey of faith. It is political and social issues that divide and separate us. These are the things that too often are used to justify schism. I encourage you to walk away from debates over issues. Choose instead to return to the teachings of Jesus that provide us with our values. It is our value system that needs to be our focus. It is our values and not issues that undergird our faith.

Here are just a few of the teachings that provide the foundation for a value system on which all other faith decisions are based. We must not forget these scriptural teachings. Many came from our Lord's own lips. *Love one another as I have loved you. Forgive your enemies and those who persecute you.* And finally, there is a specific teaching in Holy Scripture that I believe must be the foundation for all our membership and ministry decisions. *There is neither Jew nor Gentile, neither slave nor free, nor is there male and female, for you are all one in Christ Jesus.*

As you leave this House of Prayer today, I ask you to remember that you have been with a faith community that welcomes all people regardless of race, religion, gender, or sexuality. I hope that will fill you with a sense of holy pride. I hope you will be righteously proud of your church. I hope you will take pride in your Episcopal Church. This is a church that is evolving and changing, but it is a church that will continue to welcome all. There are no outcasts. Jesus welcomed all. Saint and sinner heard His teachings, received forgiveness, and were fed with the blessed loaves and fish. It is this Jesus that we follow as Episcopalians."

Once again Horace paused. He wiped the perspiration from his face with his handkerchief. His gaze swept over the congregation. "My brother and sisters in Christ, as you leave this holy place this morning, I pray above all else that you will take pride in being an Episcopal disciple of Jesus. Please, my friends, rejoice in the ministry of the Episcopal Church. Give thanks for the ministry of this parish. Take comfort knowing that we are a Church where grace and forgiveness will always trump judgmentalism."

Horace shut his eyes and bowed his head. The silence echoed off the rafters of the expansive church. Horace feared that he may have gone too far. Perhaps he'd offended some of the more traditional members. He wondered if Steele was going to be angry with his words of praise for the progress in The Episcopal Church.

Father Drummond opened his eyes in order to look out at the congregation. They were sitting frozen in their pews. Their faces were without expression. He believed their silence told him all he needed to know.

He turned to begin his descent from the pulpit. Then it was as if a spirit struck an invisible match under each person. Instantly and without warning, the worshipping congregation of First Church (Episcopal) in Falls City, Georgia rose to their feet. The gathered parish erupted in a resounding applause that lasted several minutes. It was a *Polaroid* of the renewed Episcopal Church.

The Magnolia Series

Dennis R. Maynard

CHAPTER

38

"Father Austin, I think maybe you should see these." Crystal entered his office carrying a thick manila folder. She placed them on Steele's desk.

"What are these?"

"They're requests for membership letters of transfer."

"All of these?"

"Yes, they're requests from the folks that went over to that new Anglican Church."

"Oh, that's a problem."

"Usually we'd just handle them down in the membership office, but they're so many of them."

"No, you did the right thing to bring them to me, but quite honestly, I'm not sure what to do with them. We don't issue membership transfers to protestant churches. I'm just not sure how the bishop feels about sending them over to schismatic churches. I've got to ask him. Will you please call his secretary and set up a telephone appointment? You can tell her what we need to talk about."

"In the meantime, what should I do with these?"

"How many individual transfers are in this folder?"

"There's one hundred and twenty-eight."

"Hmm, I thought there would be more."

"That's a lot."

"It is. These folks made so much noise on their way out I thought their number would be much larger. The Saturday newspaper made it sound like First Church was being gutted. That reporter suggested that there would be nothing left over here but a few old people."

"I'll set up the appointment for you. Is there any time in particular better than another?"

"No, any time."

Steele thumbed through the requests. Colonel Mitchell's

was on the top. He recognized most of the names. None of them were major contributors to First Church. He knew that most had no record of contribution whatsoever. He'd need to check with the treasurer on a few of the others. He didn't recall them being large donors, but he wasn't sure.

"Father Austin," Crystal was on the intercom. "The bishop's secretary says that he's available to receive your call now. He'd prefer you call him on his private line. He requests that you do so from yours."

"Okay."

"Do you have the bishop's private phone number?"

"Thanks, Crystal, I have it."

Steele punched in the bishop's private number.

"Steele, thanks for calling me. I trust you're on your private line."

"Yes, Sean, I am. Do you know why I'm calling?"

"My secretary advised me."

"I'm just not sure how to respond to these requests."

"We'll deal with all that in a minute. I want to know how you're handling everything."

"It's just like eating an elephant. I'm doing it one bite at a time."

"How about Randi?"

"She's really angry with the woman that tried to rape me. We're working on our options with the prosecutor."

"Health wise you're good?"

"I'm fine. It all feels so surreal."

"How about the schism? How are you handling that?"

"Horace did an extraordinary job yesterday in his sermon. He talked about the history of The Episcopal Church and just how we've evolved. He did a great job of pointing out the value system we use to address the various issues facing the Church. He also made a point of suggesting that we continue to be friends with those that have left. He said we need to respect their reasons for doing so while disagreeing with their decision."

"That all sounds great."

"It was one of his best sermons yet, but Horace is a wise and perceptive preacher. I'm so lucky to have him as a friend and partner in ministry."

"Well, if you have any problems you know where I am. You can count on me having your back."

"I know that. Every priest in this diocese knows it. That's why we are so happy to have you as our bishop."

"I'm just curious. Is that woman's husband staying with her?"

"I honestly don't know. Obviously, they've not come to Mass since it happened. Quite frankly, I hope they won't. I don't ever want to see her again. As for him, I think he's a genuinely nice guy. I really feel sorry for him. She has quite the reputation in this town. She cheated on her first husband multiple times. He didn't have a clue until he caught her. I think the most amazing thing I remember about her behavior then was that she was impervious to the potential pain she could cause him. I really believe she thought that as long as she didn't get caught he couldn't be hurt. Even after she was caught she continued to proclaim her innocence. It was incredible. I really don't know how her current husband is responding to her multiple adulteries or even this particular event. It just makes me wonder how many nice guys there are in this world that are married to sluts but don't know it."

"But Steele, my hunch is they don't see themselves as sluts."

"You're probably right. I think that in her case she has convinced herself she's a really nice person. She may even see herself as a great wife as she continues to flirt with any man that catches her eye."

"But the problem is she doesn't stop with a flirtation."

"I know. It's probably a good thing that she isn't able to see herself as she really is."

"Are you going to testify against her?"

"That's what Randi wants me to do. We're just trying to figure out a way to keep it all out of the press."

"I hadn't considered that. Gosh, that could get ugly."

"And you know who would end up paying the price?"

"Of course, it would not be the woman. You, Randi, and your children will be the focus of attention."

"And First Church."

"I know. I don't have to remind you again Steele, but I'm here if you need me."

"I know. And thank you."

"Okay, back to those requests for membership transfer. Who signed them?"

"I didn't even notice. Let me look." Steele thumbed through the requests. "They all have the same signature. He signed them as James Vernon."

The bishop roared with laughter. "You're sure?"

"Yes, the signatures are very precise. The handwriting is incredibly neat and readable."

The bishop continued to laugh.

"Sean, what's so funny?"

"Steele, catch up with me. James Vernon is also known as Jim Vernon."

"Wait! You mean your former Canon?"

"One and the same."

"Is he the rector of this new congregation?"

"That's my understanding. You'll be getting a copy of the letter from the standing committee and me in the mail. He advised us that he was leaving the Episcopal Church to become a priest in that heretical group. You'll soon receive the formal communication that he has been defrocked."

"What do you want me to do with these requests for letters of transfer?"

"We don't issue membership letters to secessionist churches. Send them all to me up here in Savannah. I'll send each of them a letter advising them what they'll have to do if they ever want to reunite with The Episcopal Church."

"That sounds good to me."

"Will their leaving hurt your congregation financially?"

"Quite frankly, I don't think it will even be noticed. None of them were major contributors and many of them contributed nothing at all."

"Well, that's the good news. In order to make their new congregation work they're going to have to come up with some money. Okay, call me if you need me."

Steele started to hang the phone up but then a thought flashed in front of him. "Wait! Sean, did I hear you correctly? James Vernon is Jim Vernon?"

"One and the same."

"Sean, is he the same one that Stone and I confronted at your office that day?"

Sean chuckled. "Oh, you're catching on."

"But Sean, isn't he gay?"

"Oh, he's so gay."

"But Sean, that new congregation has called him as their rector."

Sean continued to laugh. "And your point is?"

"One of the founding principles of their new church is that they're against ordaining gay clergy and they're opposed to gay marriage."

Sean could no longer restrain himself. He roared with laughter. When he was finally able to contain himself he chuckled, "It's all so perfect. A homophobic parish calls a closeted gay priest as their rector. You couldn't write this stuff in a novel. No one would believe it could happen. Steele, promise me that you won't tell them."

The Magnolia Series

Dennis R. Maynard

39

"I believe you know Miss Atkins from the prosecutor's office." Chief Sparks had just walked Virginia and Thackston Willoughby into one of the conference rooms at the Falls City Law Enforcement Center. "I also believe you know Mister Clemons. Mister Clemons is representing Father and Mrs. Austin."

Virginia Mudd was angry. "I am a very busy woman. I have a full day of activities scheduled. I volunteer for multiple charitable endeavors. My calendar is packed with volunteer activities today. They're all depending on me for assistance. You are preventing me from helping so many pitiful souls that require my services. Will you please tell me why you are keeping me from doing my charitable works?"

Chief Sparks glanced at the prosecutor. "I believe you can best answer that."

"Mister Willoughby, are you acting as legal counsel for your wife?"

Thackston knew why they were there. He just didn't know the extent of the evidence they had against his wife. The only thing he knew for sure was that she had lied to him about Bernice. His suspicions surrounding the event that day had run the gamut. "I am. Is my wife under arrest?"

"Not at this time."

"Then I see no reason for us to remain here. Come on, Virginia, we're leaving."

"If you leave this room, your wife will be arrested. I would advise against that. I believe you'll want to hear what we have to say."

"What crime would you charge my wife with?"

Miss Atkins took a deep breath. "Your wife will be charged immediately with possession of a date rape drug, the use of that drug against another person, and attempted rape.

That's only the beginning. If you refuse to cooperate, there are other charges that we'll bring against her."

"Thackston, what's she talking about? I don't know anything about a date rape drug. I've never tried to rape anyone." Virginia squeezed Thackston's hand. "Honey, you believe me don't you?"

"You said you have evidence? Let's see what you've got."

"Thackston, let's go. I don't want to be here." Virginia was beginning to cry.

Thackston patted her hand. He whispered in her ear. "All of this could be a bluff. Let me handle this. You need to trust me."

Virginia nodded. "Okay."

"Show me what you have."

The prosecutor slid a photo of a glass and another of some fingerprints across the table. "This is the glass of tea that your wife served to Father Austin. Our tests confirmed it contained gamma-hydroxybutyrate."

"What's that?" Virginia asked. Her voice was shaking.

"It's also known as GHB. It's a popular date rape drug."

"Thackston spent several minutes studying the photos. He compared the fingerprints."

"Thackston, I don't even know what that GH whatever is. I've never heard of it."

"Virginia, these are your fingerprints on this glass."

"Of course they are. That's one of the glasses from our house. I recognize it. Of course my fingerprints are on it."

"There are only two sets of fingerprints on that glass. It contained the drug. They're your wife's and Father Austin's. If you'll recall, your wife told us that your maid, Bernice, gave Father Austin the glass of tea. Your maid's fingerprints are not on the glass. So we know your wife lied about that."

"Is that all you have?"

"Thackston, what are you asking? I'm leaving." Virginia started to stand up. Thackston put his hand on her shoulder and pushed her back down. "We need to see everything."

Virginia protested, "I don't know what we're doing here. Thackston, why are you even listening to them?"

Thackston motioned with his hands for Virginia to be silent. "I don't believe that a glass with my wife's fingerprints on it is much of a case. I don't appreciate you calling my wife a liar. She was very upset that day. It would have been easy for her to forget just who gave the priest the glass. It's actually more logical for our maid to have served him."

Miss Atkins smiled, "But we know she didn't. Your wife gave Father Austin the glass containing the date rape drug."

"I still don't think you have much of a case."

"Maybe, if that's all that we had."

"So let's see what else you do have."

"Here is the test showing that Father Austin had GHB in his system. That's the reason he was rendered unconscious." She slid a sheet with the test result across the table.

Thackston examined the sheet. "This is still not enough to hold my wife."

Virginia let out a sigh of relief. She was so glad that Thackston was her husband and lawyer. "Does that mean we can go home?"

"We have more," Miss Atkins continued. "Here are the results of lipstick swabs we took off Father Austin's lips, neck, and chest. Here are photos of those corresponding lipstick marks on him."

Virginia was exasperated. "Of course, I left lipstick on him. I was trying to give him CPR. I was trying to breathe air into his mouth. I thought the man was dying. I was trying to save his life. I should be given a medal. Instead of that, all of you people are threatening me."

Stone Clemons started laughing, "Do you really want us to believe that you were trying to breathe air into his nipples?"

"What?" Thackston gasped.

Miss Atkins slid two more photos across the table and a corresponding test result. "The DNA in those swabs belongs to your wife."

Thackston sat back in his chair and stared at his wife.

Virginia began crying, "Thackston, they're trying to frame me. You don't believe them, do you? Honey, I would never do anything like this. I think that priest faked the entire affair. I'll bet his wife put him up to it. She's jealous of me. I know that to be fact. This is all just a setup. Please, Honey, I love you. You've got to believe me. You're the only man that I want."

"Shhh, Virginia. You'd better not say anything more. Let me handle this."

"Well, handle it!" Virginia bitterly spit the words at him.

Once again Thackston sat staring at his wife. Then he examined the evidence before him one more time. He glanced at his wife. She was sitting with her arms folded in front of her like a petulant child. "Is that all?"

"I'm afraid not." The prosecutor handed him a clear plastic bag with a long dark hair in it. "This is your wife's hair. This DNA test proves that." She shoved a photo across the table. "All of these photos were taken at the hospital and are a part of the rape kit. As you can see, that hair was lodged in the belt buckle on Father Austin's pants."

Thackston was silent. He shuffled through all the sheets and photographic evidence. "Anything else?"

"We have a transcript of the interview with your maid."

"Thackston, they're trying to frame me for something I didn't do."

"Quiet, Virginia!" Thackston raised his voice. "Do not say another word. Okay, tell me why you've not arrested my wife."

"Father and Mrs. Austin believe your wife is mentally ill. Quite frankly, they're more interested in seeing she receives psychological help. They'd like to avoid a trial."

"And they'd like to avoid all the publicity around a trial," Thackston smirked.

Stone shot back, "All of you would. I don't believe you want your wife subjected to the tabloids."

"So what are you offering?"

Miss Atkins handed Thackston a formal document. "This is a protective order signed by a judge. Your wife is to stay at least 300 yards away from Father Austin, his wife, and their children for the rest of her and their lives." Miss Atkins looked at Virginia. "Mrs. Willoughby, you need to understand that should you ever violate this protection order you will be taken into custody and go directly to jail. Violation of a protective order in the State of Georgia is a felony."

"That's it." Thackston was beginning to feel relieved.

"No." Miss Miller slid another document across the table to him. "This is a plea agreement. As you can see, it requires your wife to be admitted to a residential mental health facility of your choosing. She must remain in that facility and receive treatment until such time as her attending physician convinces our office that it is safe for her to be dismissed from treatment. If she should ever attempt to escape said facility or successfully escape the same, she will be taken into custody. This agreement will be revoked."

"And if we reject this agreement?"

"Then Chief Sparks here will arrest her. She will be taken before a judge and charged with attempted rape using GHB to incapacitate her victim. As you can see, the evidence we have is conclusive. Your wife will go to prison."

"Honey, I don't want to go to prison. I didn't do any of this. You've got to believe me. Please don't let them send me to prison."

Thackston empathized with Virginia. "I can choose the hospital?"

"You can. You will also be responsible for all the costs." Miss Atkins continued, "You need to understand that Father and Mrs. Austin can still take this case to a civil court and sue for financial damages. This plea agreement doesn't void that option."

"What if I insist on having a provision prohibiting a civil suit included in the agreement?"

"Sir, that's not going to happen," Stone was emphatic. "Clearly it's their best backup option should your wife violate this agreement. You have to take the agreement as written."

"How much time do I have to consider it?"

"This is it. The agreement will be withdrawn as soon as I leave this room." The prosecutor closed her briefcase.

Thackston watched Virginia. She was sobbing. She had her arms folded in front of her and was rocking back and forth. "I'm innocent. I would never do this. Honey, I would never be unfaithful to you. I'm a good person. I love you. I would never hurt you. You're the only man for me. I don't want any other man. I'm innocent." Then she began to babble, and sob even more. She pounded the table with her fists.

Thackston continued to watch her. He realized that his wife was having an emotional breakdown. He nodded, "I can choose the hospital?"

"Your choice." Miss Atkins agreed. "However, it must be in the continental United States. It has to be a residential hospital for the treatment of mental illness. Otherwise, the choice is completely yours. Of course, our office will want to sign off on your choice."

Stone offered in a soothing voice, "My opinion may not matter to you, but I'd make sure it was one of the best I could find."

"How much time do I have?"

"It's there in the agreement. You have seven days to get her admitted. Please understand that the Protective Order goes into effect immediately."

Thackston signed the agreement and retrieved his copy. "Let's go, Virginia. We're finished here."

Virginia utilized her most pitiful little girl's voice. "Are we going home now?"

The Magnolia Series

Dennis R. Maynard

40

Rose was standing in her kitchen. She covered her ears to block out the screams of her little son. She could hear Melvin yelling at him as he viciously beat the young boy with his belt. She knew he was using the buckle end of the belt. "God has chosen me to be your father. As your father it is my duty to see that you memorize the passages in Holy Scripture that I assign you."

Great tears rolled down Rose's face. She picked up the potholders lying on the counter and covered her ears with them. Nothing blocked out John Calvin's screams. "You will memorize these Bible passages and recite them for me each morning at breakfast or I'll beat them into you."

Rose heard her oldest son try to intervene. "Enough, Father, enough! Can't you see he's bleeding?"

"Get away from me. This is none of your concern. The Lord Jesus bled for our sins. Now this boy must bleed for his."

Rose put down the potholders and looked into the dining room. Her eldest son tried to grab Melvin's arm to stop him from beating John Calvin. Melvin swung the belt and hit her oldest son across the face with it. Blood rushed from his cheek.

Rose screamed for Melvin to stop. "You stay out of this, woman, or you'll be next." Rose grabbed the kitchen carving knife from the rack. She rushed screaming towards Melvin. She plunged the blade into his back again and again and again.

"Wake up, Rose. Wake up, you're having a nightmare." Elmer was gently shaking her awake. They were having their usual long lunch and had fallen asleep in each other's arms after making love.

"Oh God, Elmer, I had that dream again."

"Did you kill him?"

"I tried."

"Good."

"I don't think I'm ever going to be able to forgive myself for not stopping him. I let him beat my children."

"Did you really have a choice?"

"I didn't think I did back then, but I do now. I owe you, I owe Almeda, and I owe so many people for helping me realize that I am a lot stronger than I thought I was."

"Do you think you'll ever be able to let go of all that?"

"Every day it does slip farther and farther away. And then, just when I think it's all gone, that stupid dream haunts me."

"Would it help you to talk about this with Father Austin or Doctor Drummond?"

"I have talked with Father Austin about it. He thought that if I could just forgive myself it would go away."

"Have you?"

"I thought I had, but Elmer, you just can't imagine how much I hated mornings. It was the same thing over and over again. I'm afraid if Mister Clemons and Chief Sparks hadn't helped me back then, Melvin really would have killed my children. And the awful part is that I truly believe he would have believed he was doing God's work."

"How can I help you?"

Rose smiled at him and ran her fingers through his hair. "You already have. You've taught me, no, you've shown me that a real man is loving, kind, and gentle."

"I love you, Rose."

She kissed him on the cheek. "You make me feel safe. That's a feeling that I never had with him." Rose sat up in the bed. "And you make my children feel safe."

"I love them too."

"I know and I love you all the more for it."

"Rose, I'd give anything if I could magically wipe from memory all the abuse you and your children suffered at that man's hands. I know I can't, but I can give all of you a new and wonderful life."

"I love you, Elmer Idle. It's going to be a wonderful life."

"This I can promise you. Our home and our family may not be perfect, but it will be filled with love."

"And forgiveness?"

"That goes without saying. I believe that when you truly love another person forgiveness flows from that love."

"I promise you that I may not be the perfect wife, but I will make all of your other wives disappear from your memory."

"What are you talking about? Judith is the only wife I've ever had."

"See, you haven't been able to forget her. But you just wait. The day is coming when you will not remember ever being married to anyone but me."

"I will always introduce you as my wife. I will never refer to you as my second wife. You will be my only wife. And our children will not be introduced as my stepchildren. They will always be my children. I will love and care for them as my own."

"Speaking of which. Give me your hand." Rose placed Elmer's hand on her stomach. "Just wait."

Then he felt it. "Is that?"

She smiled, "I believe someone's trying to say *Hello* to their Daddy."

The Magnolia Series

Dennis R. Maynard

41

The only people in all of South Georgia that would miss a social event being hosted by Almeda Alexander Drummond were the ones not invited. Almeda personally oversaw every detail. Even when she delegated responsibilities to a chef, catering service, or event manager, the details were still subjected to her critical eye and taste buds. Most every waking hour for weeks would be devoted to planning any social occasion. Family dinners on holidays received the same scrutiny as a reception for hundreds.

Almeda was a product of the *Old South*. While she was not born to aristocracy, even the most critical observer would not know it. Her first husband, Chadsworth, had taught her well. She was an anxious student. She studied the customs of the Southern elite as thoroughly as any medical or law student studying for their final exams. She had also learned the fine art of critiquing those that did not conform. She could do so without them actually knowing what she was doing. *Bless your heart, Aren't you precious,* and *That's so niiiice,* all have a double meaning known only to true Southerners. Using those phrases at the appropriate time was simply a matter of training and practice.

The rules for hosting a Southern wedding reception were a matter of oral tradition. There were certain things that the upper classes of the Confederacy understood to be an inexcusable *faux pas.* The rules did not have to be written down. One only had to listen to the gossip and criticisms of previous receptions to learn.

The first rule should be evident but is often overlooked. The floral arrangements are not the center of attention at a Southern wedding reception. Most people won't even look at the flowers. Floral displays are reserved for the ceremony at the church. The most prominent decorative item must be the wedding cake. It should be large and mirror excellent taste. Second, an open and fully stocked bar is an essential. Almeda had made provisions for four of them. If a host dared offer anything but top-shelf liquors, there definitely would be talk. Likewise, beer and wine should be premium labels.

Third, the guests must not have to stand in line for food or drink. The only line that the guests should ever have to stand in was the receiving line. The chosen venue should be large enough to allow guests to move around. Southerners attend these events to see and be seen. They need to be able to move about freely. They will want to converse with those they deem important. Almeda had made provision for a few comfortable chairs to circle the dance floor. Again, her guests with good manners would know that these seats are reserved for the elderly and disabled.

Fourth, a groom's cake is reserved for the weddings of the lower classes. It could be considered an essential item at the weddings of trailer park trash.

The fifth dictate was the most important of all. At a Southern wedding reception the central attraction is the food. There were certain foods that were considered essential. Failure to offer those foods would be talked about for weeks following. Almeda insured that servings of pimento cheese, biscuit sandwiches, shrimp, fried green tomatoes, and okra fritters would be in plentiful supply. Running out of any food item at the reception would subject the host to the cruelest criticism one can imagine. Only poor folks run out of food at a party.

Almeda walked out of her solarium to make one final inspection before her guests arrived. The actual wedding was private and being held in the chapel at First Church. She surmised that the wedding was now over. The photographer would be taking photos. Considering drive time, she now had twenty minutes before the bridal party would arrive.

Almeda took a deep breath. The timing could not be better. The flowering trees and plants on her vast estate were in full bloom. The sweet scent from the large blossoms on her

Magnolia trees danced through the air. The wisteria hanging from her trellis added to the color and fragrance. She smiled as she noticed that her gardenia bushes were in full bloom around her pool. She stopped to inhale it all. The aroma of honeysuckle and confederate jasmine were added to the bouquet trailing into her lungs.

Almeda was pleased with everything she'd seen. She'd requested that Mary Alice Smythe assist her in overseeing the details. The waiters dressed in crisp white jackets, black ties, black pants, and well-polished black shoes were bringing the food from the kitchen and placing it on the large silver trays. Almeda had decided that only male waiters would be evident at the venue. She would keep the female *Help* in the kitchen. She told Mary Alice that these young women today just don't want to take instructions from another woman. It would just be easier to keep them in the kitchen.

"Mary Alice, you've done a wonderful job. I appreciate your assistance. Everything looks divine." Mary Alice and Almeda walked from food station to food station in the vast tent. Almeda would straighten a tray from time to time or pull on a tablecloth to straighten it, but overall everything was perfect. She decided that it wouldn't hurt to walk through the tent once more. She started at the front by the wedding cake. The pleased smile on Almeda's face suddenly turned to a frown. "Mary Alice, this tray of fried green tomatoes is half empty. And look, so is the tray of stuffed mushrooms. Didn't the staff just fill these trays?"

"Yes, I saw them. I don't know what happened." They both looked around the venue and then they spotted her at the shrimp station. She was hiding behind the ice sculpture.

With gritted teeth Almeda asked, "How on earth did she get in here?"

"She didn't come with me."

Almeda had a full head of steam going. She charged toward the ice sculpture. Mary Alice hurried to keep up with her. "Martha Dexter!" Almeda roared with anger. "What do you think you're doing?"

Martha Dexter shoved a shrimp into her mouth. She grabbed for another with each hand. She hurried to swallow. "Almeda, everything is just so good. You always have such wonderful food."

"Martha, the bridal party hasn't arrived. The reception doesn't begin until after the bride and groom arrive. You know that." Almeda was furious.

"Oh, I didn't think you'd mind if I sampled a few things ahead of time. I know you'll have plenty."

Almeda noticed that Martha was carrying an extra large handbag. "Martha, what do you have in that handbag?"

"Just my medicine. I have to keep my medications with me."

"That handbag is large enough for an entire medicine cabinet. Let me see it."

Martha pulled back, protecting her handbag. She put it behind her back. "No, this is mine."

Almeda was not about to be deterred. She was larger and stronger than Martha. She pulled the bag away from her and opened it. Inside she saw plastic bags loaded with food from the reception. "Martha, what's the meaning of this?"

"I was just going to take a few items for my Howard to enjoy tomorrow. He'll be here in a few minutes, but I thought it would be nice to have some leftovers for tomorrow."

"First, these are not leftovers. Martha, what on earth is going on with you?"

"Mary Alice, you know that Howard won't give me much money for groceries. I have to do what I can to have food for my table."

"I know," Mary Alice responded sympathetically.

Almeda would have none of it. "Martha, enough! This has got to stop. Your husband is the president and part owner of a bank. He has plenty of money."

"He tells me that he doesn't. That everything has to go back into the business."

"Give me a break. He's a member of the Country Club, he pays enormous green fees to play golf. He's a member of

The Magnolia Club. He drives a new Mercedes every other year. It appears to me there's plenty of money for what he wants."

"The household allowance he gives me doesn't cover all the expenses. There isn't enough left over for me to buy many groceries."

"Then let him sit down to an empty plate a few times. Your husband is not poor. He's greedy! He's only frugal when it comes to you or anyone else. Horace tells me that he always argues that the church staff should never receive anything but a meager cost of living raise each year. Horace also tells me he's one of the worst contributors to First Church. Your husband is not poor or frugal. He's quite generous when it comes to spending money on the things that benefit him."

A tear rolled down Martha's cheek. "What am I to do?"

Almeda studied the pitiful woman standing before her. "Martha, is that food for Howard or for you?"

Martha's voice shook as she answered, "Howard eats most all his meals at one of the clubs. After I pay the household bills there's not much left for me to eat on."

"I thought so." Almeda let out a deep breath. "Martha, you don't need to fill your handbag with food. When the reception is over I'll send you home with plenty. But Martha, you're going to have to confront Howard. He simply must give you more money. If he doesn't, then you need to leave him. The courts will make sure you have enough money to live on."

The Magnolia Series

Dennis R. Maynard

CHAPTER

42

The sitter had just arrived to watch Travis and Amanda so that Steele and Randi could attend the wedding reception. Steele heard the telephone in his study ring. He picked up the phone, "This is Father Austin."

"Steele, is this a secure line?"

He recognized the voice. He closed his study door. "It's my private line. There are no extensions. We can talk."

"Steele, I just don't know if I can do it."

"Talk to me."

Chadsworth had caught his husband, Eric, in the arms of another man. The private detective presented him with photos of the two together. "It's just so hard. I love him. I don't want to lose him, but I don't like living this way."

"Keep going."

"Steele, every time he goes out to pick up a carton of milk I fear he might be going to meet his lover. My entire body gets racked with anxiety and fear. It's so painful."

"What does he say?"

"He's so sorry. He's a fool. He knows that our love for each other will help us get through this."

"Do you believe him?"

"I want to."

"Have you forgiven him?"

"I'm trying."

"Tell me about his contrition."

"There have been tears. He begs me to forgive him."

"Is there something in particular you need to hear from him?"

"I really don't know what I need. I'm just having such a difficult time trusting him again."

"Of course you are. He destroyed that trust. It can't be

built back in a few days or months."

"He's going to go to his family reunion down in Newport Beach."

"And?"

"I'm filled with suspicion. Is he really going to a family reunion? Or does he plan to meet up with his stud while he's there?"

"Can you go with him?"

"It's not an option. His family doesn't know he's gay."

"Huh?"

"They're old country Germans. They would disown him if they found out. I do know that's fact."

"Does he understand he needs to rebuild your trust?"

"We've not talked about that in particular."

"Maybe you should. The responsibility for earning your trust rests totally on him. He needs to understand that the slightest secret or the smallest lie causes you to trust him even less."

"I hadn't thought about using those words to describe what I need."

"What would happen if you described your feelings that way?"

"I'm willing to give it a try."

"Do you still have the photos the detective took?"

"My attorney insisted on keeping them. If we were to get a divorce, he can use them against Eric if he were to plead innocence for financial gain."

"Do you spend a lot of time thinking about the two of them?"

"It's hard not to. Steele, can you imagine just how much it hurts to see the person you love naked and in the arms of another?"

"I know how much it hurts to suspect that possibility. I can't even imagine the pain of actually having photographic evidence."

"Trust me on this one, you don't ever want to."

"This is what I know about forgiveness. If you trust that

your partner is genuinely sorry and they are doing all they can to rebuild your trust, you have to put the event behind you and leave it there."

"What are you saying?"

"I'm saying you have to leave the past in the past."

"I think that's easier said than done."

"It is, but it's the only way to move on with your life and your relationship."

"I understand. But first I need to work on getting him to help me learn to trust him."

"Chadsworth, here's the bad news. You'll eventually be able to put the past in the past. But there's always going to be some event, place, odor, song, the list is endless that may stimulate that memory in you again. All the fear and anxiety will wash over you yet one more time. Even then you have to push it out of your mind."

"I don't know if I want to live that way."

"And that, my friend, is the reason that adultery has destroyed most every marriage it has impacted. It's not for the lack of forgiveness. It's the pain of having to live with the memory. The primary stimulus for that pain is looking at the person that hurt you. If your mind keeps returning to that person's betrayal, or as they say *the scene of the crime*, it will bring the pain back to you."

"So you're saying either I learn to live with it or I divorce him."

"I think you need to explain it to him exactly that way. You will try to forgive him the first time, but if he ever does it again your relationship is over. You have to say it, but you also have to mean it."

"This is what I know. If I have to spend hours or days wondering what he's up to when he's not with me, I choose to end it."

"That takes us back to him. He needs to understand that. He needs to work on rebuilding your trust."

The Magnolia Series

Dennis R. Maynard

CHAPTER

43

The elite class in the *Old South* would never consider not having a receiving line. The proper etiquette for a receiving line has been handed down from generation to generation. It's second nature to every Southern gentleman and lady. First up in the receiving line are the people paying for and hosting the reception. Most often these are the parents of the bride, but not always. Standing immediately next to them will be the bride and groom. The groom's parents stand on the other side of the groom. If the grandparents of the bridal couple are present, they are positioned next in the line. On occasion great-grandparents will follow. If there is a wealthy aunt or uncle that has recently given the couple a house, automobile, or furniture for their new love nest, they may also be included. If the best man and maid of honor are close family, they may stand at the end of the line.

The placement of the receiving line must be thought through carefully. The goal is to allow all the guests to move through the line quickly. There should be plenty of room to allow this to happen. Guests waiting to process through the receiving line need to be protected from inclement weather.

Well-bred Southerners know that a receiving line is not the time for extended conversation. Courtesies are restricted to a handshake, a greeting, and on occasion an introduction. To the bride's parents and/or the host of the reception, the guest shakes their hand and thanks them for inviting them. Guests shake the bride's hand only if it has been extended. The proper greeting for the bride is *Best Wishes*. Shaking the groom's hand is always appropriate. The proper greeting in his case is *Congratulations*.

It's acceptable to compliment the bride by telling her that she looks *absolutely beautiful* or *lovely* even if she could pass as the bride of Frankenstein. It is also acceptable to tell the groom *you're a lucky man* even while thinking *you poor sap, you have no idea what you've just done.*

The socially elite know that receiving line hugs and kisses are inappropriate. Without exception a make-up artist was employed to paint the faces on all the female members of the wedding party. Hugs and kisses run the risk of smudging the artist's work or dislodging the bridal veil. Hugs and kisses are shared after the dancing has begun.

The receiving line at Rose and Elmer's reception was unusually short so it moved quickly. Horace and Almeda were first in line. Almeda stood next to Rose. She was in the best position to introduce most all of the guests present to the bride and groom.

The reception flowed smoothly. Almeda and Mary Alice kept a critical eye on all the tables to make sure that the food trays were quickly and efficiently replenished. Mary Alice became concerned when she noticed Martha Dexter standing in line at a couple of the bars. She quietly passed the word to all four bartenders to water the drinks of the lady dressed in that God-awful purple dress with feathers in her hat.

"Almeda, the corn pone sliders are a real hit. Weren't they a lot of work?"

"I could have used biscuits or just plain cornbread, but Horace encouraged me to go all the way and prepare my corn pone recipe."

"There's something different about yours. If you don't mind my asking, what did you add?"

"I don't mind at all. I added grease from some salt pork to the batter. I also made sure that the cooks used cast iron skillets to fry them."

"How did you decide on brisket?"

She smiled, "It was trial and error. I tried several different meats for Horace to taste. It wasn't until I added some melted cheese to the brisket that his eyes lit up. He assured me that the men present would love it. He called it *man food.*" The two ladies rolled their eyes at each other and chuckled.

"Men!" Mary Alice snorted.

Almeda had allowed exactly one hour after the last guest moved through the receiving line for consuming food and drink. She approached Steele Austin, "I think now would be a good time for your toast."

Steele and Randi walked to the elevated stage at the far end of the tent. The band was sitting quietly behind then. The area prepared as a dance floor was immediately in front of them. Randi stood at his side. The waiters were moving quickly through the crowd with silver trays containing glasses filled with champagne. When it appeared all the guests had been served, Steele tapped on the microphone and cleared his throat. "Ladies and gentlemen, may I have your attention? I'd like to make a toast to the bride and groom. Rose and Elmer, will you please join us?"

Once Rose and Elmer were standing with them, Steele began his toast. "Rose and Elmer, the Christian story is a story of betrayal, death, and resurrection. On Good Friday Jesus was betrayed and met His death. But God had other plans. Just three days later he was raised to a new and beautiful life. As I was thinking about your love story I saw a lot of similarities. You had your own Good Fridays. There was the betrayal and death of your previous relationships. You each could have lingered in your pain and unhappiness, but God had another plan for you. It all began when Elmer walked into an alteration shop. Little did he realize that day his life and the life of that seamstress were going to be altered. From betrayal and death, God has given you a new and wonderful life filled with love. Ladies and gentlemen, please lift your glasses and join with me in wishing God's blessings on the new and improved Mister and Mrs. Elmer Idle."

There were several *hear hears* shouted out over the sound of tinkling glasses. In his deep baritone voice Horace Drummond shouted, "Thanks be to God."

Rose spoke into the microphone. "We'd like to have my children join us here on the stage." When her three children were with them, Rose continued. "Elmer and I have a gift for you." She took the papers that Randi was holding and gave one copy to each child. Rose fought back her tears. "Thanks to Mister Stone Clemons we were able to expedite these papers. Children, these are the papers signed by a judge that state that Elmer has now legally adopted you. All of your last names have been changed to *Idle*."

The children screamed and ran to Elmer and threw their arms around him. John Calvin shouted, "Does this mean we can call you *Daddy*?" The room exploded with applause as Elmer, Rose, and their children dissolved in happy tears. Most all the guests watching the scene fought back the water welling up in their own eyes. Almeda allowed her tears to flow freely.

When the Idle family regained their composure, Steele once again asked for the guests to silence their conversation. "Ladies and gentlemen, it is now time for Mister and Mrs. Idle to have their first dance as husband and wife. Mister Idle has chosen the song for their first dance. He wanted to surprise his bride. It's a song that most of us will remember was made popular by Bobby Vinton."

As the orchestra began the introduction to the song, Elmer twirled Rose out onto the dance floor. The soloist began to sing,

> *Roses are red my love,*
> *violets are blue,*
> *sugar is sweet my love,*
> *but not as sweet as you.*

Once again, applause filled the tent as the newly wed couple danced.

Mary Alice's eyes widened, "I didn't realize that Rose knew how to dance."

Almeda smiled, "She's been taking lessons. They both have."

Mary Alice took a second look at Rose. "Hmm Almeda, this is the first time I've had a chance to look at her full profile. Do I see what I think I see?"

Another tear rolled down Almeda's cheek. She nodded, "I'm so happy for them. They're going to have a little girl."

The Magnolia Series

Dennis R. Maynard

CHAPTER

44

The Respite By the Sea in Santa Barbara, California looks more like a luxury resort than a psychiatric hospital. It is small, exclusive, and expensive. The eighteen suites are comfortably furnished *with queen size beds, mahogany side tables, a dresser, and a chest.* Each living area has French doors that look out on the blue Pacific. The living areas boast an overstuffed couch and chairs. There is an electric fireplace in each. A fifty-inch television is mounted on the wall. The bathroom is beautifully tiled and furnished with a *Jacuzzi* tub and a separate steam shower. Meals can be taken in the common dining room or ordered through the twenty-four hour room service. Residents may also have their meals or snacks brought in through a delivery service that many of the finer restaurants utilize.

The therapy options are plentiful and geared toward the individual patient's interests. Popular choices incorporate meditation, yoga, massage, acupuncture, art, and music. Patients may also choose to have a golf outing or equine therapy included in their treatment plan.

Virginia Willoughby had spent the entire week before her admittance pleading with Thackston. "I've not done the things they're accusing me of doing. They've manufactured all that evidence. It's not true. I would never do anything like that. I'll bet it's all Almeda's fault. She hates me. She's the one behind it. She paid off the priest to pretend to pass out. I'll bet he didn't even pass out. It was all a ruse. If I could just talk to him I know we could straighten this out. I know he likes me. He's always been so nice to me."

The more she pleaded and the more she tried to rewrite the entire event, the more convinced Thackston was that his wife truly was ill.

"Can't you get these charges dismissed? You're one

214

of the best attorneys in the state. You're my husband. Surely you're not going to bow to that female prosecutor. You're so much smarter than she is." He finally had to remind her of the ultimatum included in the plea agreement. Either she agreed to be admitted to the hospital or she'd be going to prison. Those were her only two options.

The only time that he felt like he was able to reason with her concerned her treatment. "Virginia, the plea bargain states that you can come back home once the doctors have convinced the prosecutor that you're well. You need to cooperate fully with your psychiatrist so that he'll declare you healed as soon as possible."

Thackston knew that *The Respite* pleasantly surprised Virginia. She found her suite to be much more than she had expected. Virginia was awestruck when she spotted one of her favorite movie stars. The actress had checked herself into the hospital and was being treated for depression.

Virginia was also pleased to see that there were no walls, no security gates, and that she could leave any time she chose. Once again, Thackston had to caution her. "Virginia, if you leave you'll be signing your own arrest warrant. Do not leave. Stay here until the doctor says you can leave. I will come visit as often as my caseload allows. One more thing, Virginia, do not try to contact Father Austin or his wife by phone, mail, or carrier pigeon. They are strictly off limits. Do you understand?"

"Yes, Thackston. I'm not an idiot. Do you still love me?"

"Virginia, I must love you or I wouldn't be going through all of this with you. I'm doing what I think needs to be done. I want you to get well. I want you to come back home." He kissed her on the forehead and left.

Virginia unpacked her bags and put her clothing in the chest and closet. She complained to the receptionist that the hospital didn't provide her with proper *Help* to unpack her bags for her. She went into the bathroom and put all her makeup on the dressing table. She turned on the cosmetic mirror that came with the room. She studied her face carefully. She was pleased with what she saw staring back at her. Virginia thumbed through the fashion magazines that Thackston had purchased for her at the airport gift shop. She realized she was already bored. Her first session with the psychiatrist was still two hours away.

She walked through the open French doors and out onto her patio. The grassy knoll in front of the patio led down to the sandy beach. She walked to the water's edge. She listened to the waves and watched the seagulls. She took her shoes off and waded into the water. She was surprised at just how cold the water was. It wasn't anything like the warm waters of the Gulf of Mexico that wash up on the Florida and Georgia shores.

Virginia returned to her room. She used the remote to turn on her television. After channel surfing for an hour or so she turned it off. She spotted a leather notebook on the desk. She opened it and read through the list of restaurant menus included in it. She spotted a sushi bar's offerings. She picked up the telephone and called the restaurant. "Do you deliver?"

"Yes, we do."

"Do you deliver to *The Respite*?"

"Yes, for the usual delivery charge."

Virginia placed her order. "How long will it be?"

"We are only a few blocks away. We should be there in fifteen or twenty minutes."

When her doorbell rang, Virginia's breath was taken away. The delivery boy was tall, tan, and muscular. His long blonde hair flowed freely over his shoulders. He was the epitome of a *California Surfer*. He could have easily adorned any magazine cover.

He smiled and revealed a mouth full of pearly white teeth. "Are you Mrs. Willoughby?"

Virginia drank in the beautiful specimen standing before her. She finally managed to answer him. "Yes, come in. I need to get my handbag."

The surfer entered and stood by the door while she opened her wallet. A familiar smell floated through the room.

She walked back to him and unapologetically sniffed his chest. "Oh, I see you don't just deliver sushi. What else do you have on you?"

His face blushed a bright red. Then he smiled, "I'm not sure I know what you're talking about."

"Oh, I think you do." Virginia ran her fingers up his shirt and began pulling the buttons back to open it.

"Hey, stop."

Virginia looked up at the handsome specimen and gave him her most seductive smile. She continued to unbutton his shirt.

"Lady, are you sure you know what you're doing?"

Virginia kissed his chest and then his lips. She took him by the hand and pulled him toward her bedroom. "You're about to get the tip of your life."

She drew the smoke from the marijuana cigarette deep into her lungs. She then handed it back to the naked surfer lying next to her. "What's your name?"

"Rick."

"Well Rick, I'm going to be in this hotel for some time. I'm going to need to eat a lot of sushi. Do you think you can handle that?"

He smiled at her and then pulled her on top of him for a second time. "What do you think?"

Virginia glanced at the clock on her side table. "Damn," she grunted. "I'm going to miss my first doctor's appointment." She closed her eyes so she could focus on her own pleasure.

The Magnolia Series

Dennis R. Maynard

Epilogue

It was Steele Austin's favorite time of the year in South Georgia. The dogwoods and azaleas were in full bloom. From his office he could look out on the historic First Church Cemetery. From time to time a breeze would pick up one of the white dogwood blossoms and gently wave it in the air. Like a feather floating in the wind the blossom would then lightly fall to the ground. The colorful trees and plants framed First Church. That was a picture in itself. Visiting artists could often be seen this time of the year standing at their easels painting the scene as it unfolded.

Several weeks have now passed since the schismatic group left First Church. There had been a minimal dip in Sunday attendance, but if last Sunday was any indication the drop was temporary. Financially, there had been no impact at all. The greatest benefit was felt in the congregation itself. Mary Alice Smythe remarked after last Sunday's early Mass, "Mister Austin, since that group left to start their own church even the bricks in this building are breathing easier."

Steele could tell the difference. The usual complainers no longer passed through his door. His morning mail was not littered with *suggestions* for self-improvement. The staff also appeared to be more relaxed. He often heard laughter coming from their offices. He mused as to whether or not the peace of the church could be so easily restored. If a few antagonists are removed or remove themselves, is that all it takes? Can a handful of loudmouth complainers poison the ministry of an entire congregation? As quickly as he asked the questions of himself he knew the answers. It was evident all around him. Peace may not yet be restored to Jerusalem, but First Church was enjoying a peace he'd not known since he walked through the doors twelve years ago.

Not a single member had said anything to him about the new *Integrity* group. He and Randi attended their first potluck dinner. Twenty-four other people were present. Steele was pleased to see a few people that had only attended First Church on Christmas Eve. It was a pleasant evening. The food and drinks were wonderful and beautifully presented. The conversations were pleasant. Everyone expressed gratitude to Randi and to him for being there. One gentleman, a former manager of *Rich's Department Store* in Atlanta, took a special liking to Randi. He wanted to make a shopping date with her.

There was no talk of protests or petitions. There was general agreement that a *Pride Parade* was not a realistic possibility in Falls City, but they could march in the parade in Atlanta with the Episcopal contingent. A couple of the men asked Steele why incense couldn't be used every Sunday at one of the Masses. Another couple wanted to donate an icon of Saint Sebastian to First Church. Saint Sebastian was martyred in the early part of the third century. There is an abundance of homoerotic art surrounding him. For that reason alone, it is commonly accepted that he is the patron saint of gay and lesbian Christians. Steele told them the church would joyfully accept their gift.

Steele was handed three new pledge cards at the dinner. Each person told him that they loved coming to First Church, but they'd never felt included enough to financially support the parish. When Steele examined the pledge cards before giving them to the treasurer, his eyes bulged. Two of those pledges were now the largest on record at First Church.

"Father Austin," the maintenance supervisor interrupted his thoughts. He was standing at Steele's open door. "Do you have a minute?"

"Sure, come on in."

"If you're free, I need to show you something out there in the churchyard."

Steele followed him past the church and down to the oldest part of the cemetery. "I wanted to show you this old magnolia tree."

Steele looked up at the tree. "Wow, that tree is huge! How big is it?"

"I'm guessing seventy or eighty feet. It's the largest tree

in the churchyard."

"What's that growing on it?"

"That's powdery mildew. It's actually caused by a little insect."

"Will it kill the tree?"

"Yes sir, it will."

"Can you stop it?"

"If I spray it in the next couple of weeks I can, but if I don't spray it in the next ten to fourteen days it'll die. The little insects will develop a coat of armor. No poison can penetrate their hard shell."

"So what's the problem?"

"It's the vestryman in charge of the cemetery."

"You mean Howard Dexter?"

"Yes sir. Mister Dexter won't let me spend any of the money in the maintenance budget to buy the poison. He told me to just cut the tree down."

Steele studied the gravestones surrounding the tree. He noticed that some of the death dates on the markers were from the late 1700s, 1800s and the early 1900s.

The maintenance supervisor once again interrupted his thoughts. "This old tree has been standing guard over these folks' remains for close to a hundred years. It's the oldest tree in this churchyard. There's a good chance that one or more of those sleeping souls were here when this tree was planted."

Steele nodded and looked back at the tree. He turned around to take in this entire section of the cemetery. "I don't get down here very often. There are no available gravesites here. Most of the interments I have to do are up there in the new section."

"Yes sir."

Steele turned so that he could view the area around the tree one more time. "Is this the only magnolia tree in this section of the cemetery?"

"Yes sir."

His thoughts drew to a rapid conclusion. "I have a little money in my discretionary fund. I'll give it to you to buy the chemicals to treat this tree. We don't need any of Howard Dexter's maintenance money. Let's save this tree for all the people sleeping in her shadow. Until the trumpet sounds, the tree will continue to serve her purpose. It would be a shame to let her die after all these years. Let her live. She's the last magnolia!"

The Magnolia Series

Dennis R. Maynard

ABOUT THE AUTHOR

After four decades of parish ministry, The Reverend Doctor Dennis R. Maynard retired in 2005 to expand his consulting and writing ministry within the larger Church. Since his retirement, he has worked with the bishops, clergy, schools, and leadership in the congregations of thirty-two dioceses in the United States and Canada. He has become the best selling author of nineteen books. Several of his books are used extensively in the congregations and theological schools of several denominations in Canada, England, the United States, and beyond.

Over 250,000 new and lifelong Episcopalians have read *Those Episkopols.* 3,500 congregations throughout the United States routinely utilize the book in their evangelism and new member ministries. Several denominational leaders have called *Those Episkopols* the "unofficial handbook for *The Episcopal Church*". Two Presiding Bishops of the Episcopal Church have stated that it should be required reading for every Episcopalian.

He is also the author of *Forgive and Get Your Life Back.* Numerous clergy use that particular book to do forgiveness training in their counseling ministries and with small groups in their congregations.

Maynard has written a series of novels focusing on life in the typical congregation. The ten books in this series of novels have received popular acceptance from both clergy and lay people. Readers anxiously await each new chapter in *The Magnolia Series.*

"These novels give us a chance to look at the underside of parish life. The story lines are fictional. However, readers invariably think they recognize the characters. If not, they know someone just like the folks that attend First Church (Episcopal) in the town of Falls City, Georgia."

His book, *When Sheep Attack,* is based on twenty-five case studies of clergy that were attacked by a small group of misguided antagonists in their congregations. The documented cases illustrate the methods that the antagonists used to successfully remove their senior pastor, leaving the congregations divided and crippled. The book reveals how it happened, what could have been done to stop it, and what can be done to prevent it from happening to your pastor and parish.

He has since written two additional books on the subject that have rapidly become best sellers. *Preventing A Sheep Attack* is being used to guide boards to establish mechanisms to prevent an attack. *Healing For Pastors and People Following A Sheep Attack* has brought comfort and healing to hundreds that have endured that nightmare. Faculty in several theological schools in America, Canada, and other countries use these three books as resource materials in their classes.

Doctor Maynard served some of the largest congregations in *The Episcopal Church* in America. His ministry included congregations in South Carolina, Oklahoma, Illinois, Texas, and California. President George H.W. Bush and his family were faithful members of the congregation he served in Houston, Texas. It is the largest congregation in *The Episcopal Church.*

He has served other notable leaders that represent the diversity of his ministry. These national leaders include a former Secretary of State, James Baker; Former Secretary of Education, Richard Riley; Supreme Court Nominee, Clement Haynsworth; and the infamous baby doctor, Benjamin Spock, among others.

Doctor Maynard maintains an extensive travel schedule. He is frequently called on to speak and lead retreats. He has also consulted with parishes, schools, dioceses, and religious organizations throughout the United States and Canada.

He was ordained a priest at the age of twenty-four. His first assignments were as the curate at Grace Church and vicar of Saint Philip's Mission in Muskogee, Oklahoma. The bishop of the diocese charged him with closing Saint Philip's Mission, an African American congregation. He was to merge it with Grace Church. At the close of his first year, the merger was realized.

Doctor Maynard received a call to be vicar of Saint Mark's Mission in Dallas, Texas. In less than a year, the mission achieved parish status. The next year, he successfully led the merger of that parish with nearby Saint Margaret's Parish in Richardson, Texas. The combined congregations chose the name Church of the Epiphany. Over the next eight years, they grew to a parish averaging one thousand people in attendance at five Sunday services, including a service in Mandarin.

Father Maynard led the congregation to conduct three capital campaigns. One campaign was held to build a new church with a pipe organ, another to remodel the old nave into a parish hall, and a capital campaign to build a parish life center.

The congregation started a counseling center, a bookstore, and a preschool. The parish also became one of the treatment centers for a teen drug abuse program. The congregation partnered with an African American congregation in South Dallas to form a block partnership. The Epiphany congregation brought two large refugee families from Viet Nam to Richardson. They helped them begin new and productive lives.

Epiphany parish was recognized for its growth and ministry in a 1978 article in *The Episcopalian,* the national newspaper for *The Episcopal Church.*

At the age of thirty-four, Maynard was called to historic Christ Church and School in Greenville, South Carolina. At the time, it was listed as the seventh largest parish congregation in *The Episcopal Church.* Under his leadership, it grew to be the fourth largest with six Sunday services.

During his tenure, the congregation set up five not for profit corporations. Each one administered a Food Bank, a soup kitchen, a free medical clinic, a safe house for abused women, and a house for homeless men living with HIV and AIDS. The parish also built four Habitat For Humanity houses while he was rector. Along with the diocese, the people of Christ Church worked with the Bishop of Haiti on several projects to meet the needs of the people of that diocese. The parish established a preschool, a bookstore, and a counseling center under his leadership.

When Maynard went to Greenville, Christ Church Episcopal School was in decline. The school was being heavily subsidized by the parish budget. This was negatively impacting the growth and ministry programs in the congregation. Conversations were held among the leadership about closing the upper school. There were more students withdrawing from the upper school than were actually enrolling in it. Maynard and the head of school at the time began an aggressive new student recruitment program and marketing campaign. Together, they established a board of visitors and an annual fund for the school. The decline reversed after five years, and the school began to grow.

Maynard led two capital campaigns to expand and improve the facilities for the parish and school at the downtown campus and broke ground for a new middle school building. The campaigns allowed for the renovation and expansion of the downtown campus property. The diocese had made the decision to close one of the mission churches in Greenville. He asked the bishop to make it a chapel of the parish to see if the decline in membership couldn't be turned around. Saint Andrew's congregation became a self-supporting parish in just three years.

Maynard left Christ Church to become the Vice Rector of the largest congregation in *The Episcopal Church*, Saint Martin's in Houston, Texas. While at Saint Martin's, he was able to establish *The Seabury Institute Southwest*. It was the first regional campus for Seabury Western Theological Seminary in Chicago, Illinois. Clergy were able to study and earn advanced degrees in congregational development through the institute.

The bishop and calling committee of Saint James by the Sea in La Jolla, California approached Father Maynard about becoming their rector. The bishop of the diocese and vestry at the time were concerned about the decline in attendance, membership, and the finances of the parish.

The parish was bleeding its endowment for daily operations and was quite literally living from bequest to bequest. Doctor Maynard believed himself called to be their rector. He was instrumental in discovering and convicting a long-time employee of the parish that had been embezzling large sums of money. Father Maynard worked with the vestry leaders to establish internal controls and audits. The new procedures were designed to safeguard the finances and prevent a reoccurrence. They established a separate governing board to safeguard the endowment of the parish. The pledge budget tripled in just three years. During Maynard's tenure, the parish was able to start an operating reserve to meet projected obligations.

The congregation experienced rapid growth that routinely filled four Sunday services to capacity. A successful bookstore and gift shop was established. He led a capital campaign to address the deferred maintenance issues. The plan included provisions for making the property accessible to persons living with physical disabilities. The turnaround at St. James by the Sea was featured in an article in an international Anglican Magazine.

Doctor Maynard's ministry has included service on several diocesan boards and committees. These included multiple program committees in his dioceses, director of summer camps for boys, diocesan trustee, finance committees, and executive committees. He was elected Regional Dean of various diocesan deaneries on several occasions. He served on the Cursillo secretariat and was spiritual director for the Cursillo Movement multiple times. Maynard served as co-chair for two diocesan capital campaigns.

He served multiple terms on the board of the National Association of Episcopal Schools. For twelve years he served as a trustee on the board of Seabury Western Theological Seminary. Father Maynard was appointed as an adjunct professor in congregational development at Seabury. He was the co-coordinator for two national leadership conferences designed for large congregations with multiple staff ministries.

Doctor Maynard was twice named to *Oxford's Who's Who.* It is also known as *The Elite Registry of Extraordinary Professionals.* He was named twice to *Who's Who Among Outstanding Americans.*

Maynard completed two undergraduate degrees. He was awarded an Associate of Arts Degree in psychology and chemistry. A divisional major in the social sciences that included studies in psychology, sociology, history, and a minor in biology earned him a Bachelor of Arts Degree. He earned a Masters Degree in theology from Seabury Western Theological School. His Doctor of Ministry Degree was also earned in Chicago at Seabury Western.

Doctor Maynard and his wife, Nancy Anne, reside in Rancho Mirage, California.

**

OTHER BOOKS BY DENNIS R. MAYNARD

THOSE EPISKOPOLS
This is a popular resource for clergy to use in their new member ministries. It seeks to answer the questions most often asked about The Episcopal Church. Questions like: "Can You Get Saved in the Episcopal Church?" "Why Do Episcopalians Reject Biblical Fundamentalism?" "Does God Like All That Ritual?" "Are There Any Episcopalians in Heaven?" And others.

FORGIVEN, HEALED AND RESTORED
This book makes a distinction between forgiving those who have injured us and making the decision to reconcile with them or restore them to their former place in our lives.

THE MONEY BOOK
The primary goal of this book is to present some practical teachings on money and Christian Stewardship. It also encourages the reader not to confuse their self-worth with their net worth.

FORGIVE AND GET YOUR LIFE BACK
This book teaches the forgiveness process to the reader. It's a popular resource for clergy and counselors to use to do forgiveness training. In this book, a clear distinction is made between forgiving, reconciling, and restoring the penitent person to their former position in our lives.

WHEN SHEEP ATTACK
Your rector is bullied, emotionally abused, and then his ministry is ended. Your parish is left divided. Many faithful members no longer attend. This book is based on the case studies of twenty-five clergy who had just such an experience.

What could have been done? What can you do to keep it from happening to you and your parish? Discussion questions are included that make it suitable for study groups.

PREVENTING A SHEEP ATTACK

This is a book that clergy and lay leaders can use to train and educate their leadership on ways to prevent a sheep attack. It explains why allowing a sheep attack to occur means that it is inevitable that someone will be ejected from the congregational system.   He explains why parish and denominational leaders must choose.

HEALING FOR PASTORS & PEOPLE AFTER A SHEEP ATTACK

If you are a wounded senior minister, music minister, minister of education, or faithful lay leader that still suffers with the pain inflicted on you by a handful of antagonists, this book will assist you with your healing. Years later, if you still wake in a cold sweat shaking from a nightmare filled with abusive memories, this book can help you. If you feel empty spiritually and unappreciated by the very Church you felt called to serve, this book will comfort you.

EVEN JESUS NEEDED MONEY

In this, his seventeenth book, Doctor Maynard has once again written with pastors and lay leaders in mind. This is a resource they can use in premarital counseling, marital counseling, with youth, and small groups. This conversation guide on money and stewardship raises the following questions, among others.

Do You Pay Everyone But Yourself?
Are Your Children Becoming Financial Snowflakes?
What Type of Giver Are You?
Are All Charities Equal?
Are The Wealthy Blessed or Just Lucky?

THE MAGNOLIA SERIES

BEHIND THE MAGNOLIA TREE (BOOK ONE)

Meet The Reverend Steele Austin. He is a young Episcopal priest who receives an unlikely call to one of the most prestigious congregations in the Southern United States. Soon his idealism conflicts with the secrets of sex, greed, and power at Historic First Church. His efforts to minister to those living with AIDS and HIV bring him face to face with members of the Klu Klux Klan. Then one of the leading members seeks his assistance in coming to terms with the double life he's been living. The ongoing conflict with the bigotry and prejudice that are in the historic fabric of the community turn this book into a real page-turner.

WHEN THE MAGNOLIA BLOOMS (BOOK TWO)

In this the second book in the Magnolia Series, Steele Austin finds himself in the middle of a murder investigation. In the process, the infidelity of one of his closest priest friends is uncovered. When he brings an African American priest on the staff, those antagonistic to his ministry find even more creative methods to rid themselves of the young idealist. Then a most interesting turn of events changes the African priest's standing in the parish. A misguided young associate undermines the rector by preaching a gospel of hate, alienating most of the women in the congregation and all the gay and lesbian members. The book closes with a cliffhanger that will leave the reader wanting another visit to Falls City, Georgia.

PRUNING THE MAGNOLIA (BOOK THREE)

Steele Austin's vulnerability increases even further when he uncovers a scandal that will shake First Church to its very foundation. In order to expose the criminal, he must first prove his own innocence. This will require him to challenge his very own bishop. The sexual sins of the wives of one of the parish leaders present a most unlikely pastoral opportunity for the rector. In the face of the ongoing attacks of his antagonists, Father Steele Austin is given the opportunity to leave First Church for a thriving parish in Texas.

THE PINK MAGNOLIA (BOOK FOUR)

The Rector's efforts to meet the needs of gay teenagers that have been rejected by their own families cast a dark cloud over First Church. A pastoral crisis with an antagonist transforms their relationship from enemies to friends. The Vestry agrees to allow the Rector to sell the church-owned house and purchase his own, but not all in the congregation approve. The reader is given yet another view of church politics. This particular book ends with the most suspense-filled cliffhanger yet.

THE SWEET SMELL OF MAGNOLIA (BOOK FIVE)

The fifth book in the Magnolia Series follows the Rector's struggle with trust and betrayal in his own marriage. His suspicions about his wife take a heavy toll on his health and his ministry. In face of the congregation's objections, he chooses to bring a woman priest on the staff. Some reject her ministry totally. Then the internal politics of the Church are exposed even further with the election of a Bishop. Those with their own agenda manipulate the election itself. Just when you think the tactics of those opposed to the ministry of Steele Austin can't go any lower, they do.

THE MAGNOLIA AT SUNRISE (BOOK SIX)

The lives of The Reverend Steele Austin and the people of First Church face new challenges. Father Austin takes his sabbatical time to examine his life's purpose. Still stinging from the most recent attacks on his wife and himself from the antagonists in his parish, he wrestles with the decision as to whether or not he wants to return to First Church. He is even uncertain if he wants to remain in the priesthood.

THE CHANGING MAGNOLIA (BOOK SEVEN)

The masters of the great plantations ruled over those they believed to be inferior to them. Their descendants often believe they are entitled to this same position. With divine right, they appeal to their wealth and bloodline, demanding that the less important in their world be subservient to them. In

Falls City, Georgia, the elite born to positions of superiority utilize intimidation, slander, blackmail, sex, and even murder to get their way. In this seventh visit to Historic First Church, these powerful people have used their influence to destroy the spirit of their own pastor and his family.

THE MAGNOLIA AT CHRISTMAS (BOOK EIGHT)

All the characters that the readers have loved return to Falls City and First Church for Christmas. Their holiday celebration will bring a smile to your face, an occasional chuckle, and most certainly a tear. Christmas is a happy time in Falls City. You'll want to celebrate it at First Church. It ends with one of the biggest shocks and surprises yet.

THE MESSY MAGNOLIA (BOOK NINE)

The twists and turns in this book will remind faithful readers just why they are fans of the characters that reside in Falls City, Georgia. Virginia Mudd is out of prison and has her lustful eyes focused on a certain priest. The bishop's sexual identity is being threatened at the same time he falls in love with a most unlikely prospect. The antagonists continue their efforts to undermine the rector. And Almeda Alexander Drummond, well, once again you'll remember why you love to hate her. The Epilogue in this book will send you to the mailbox with letters demanding Book Ten.

THE LAST MAGNOLIA (BOOK TEN)
TO BE RELEASED IN 2019

www.Episkopols.com

Visit Amazon.com to discover Doctor Maynard's books that are on Kindle.

WWW.EPISKOPOLS.COM

Books for Clergy and the People They Serve

Made in the USA
Coppell, TX
28 June 2022

79365334R00129